Half Blood

AN KIM

Chapter One

P eople line the streets on both sides, cheering raucously as we make out way toward the city gates. I realized that Songak was big two weeks ago when I arrived and got my first glimpse of those massive stone walls. Seeing the sheer number of people crowding the main road to see us off now, I correct my initial assessment. The city is enormous and filled to the brim with people.

My grey mare flicks an ear nervously at the crowd, though she keeps steady behind Tama's sorrel stallion a few steps ahead. I grip the reins in one hand while I alternate between watching the backs of my friends ahead of me and examining the citizens that have come to wish us luck.

The difference between us halfings and the humans has never been clearer than right now when they stand there in their homespun and linens, work-worn and weary from daily lives. And we ride past in flashy silks and glittering jewels, straight-backed and unflinching.

You'd never guess that the twelve of us in today's party were born in mud and bamboo houses. That we were raised on the same rice patties and played in nothing but rayon sashes in the dirt with our human neighbors. Now we look like royalty, like the immortals we were bred to be, and we have to continue breeding. We have to look imposing and impenetrable. We can't be anything else today.

It's a hunting party, but no one has to die today. Probably. The goal isn't death, it's reproduction. We're leaving to find our mates. Though "find" is a rather mild way of putting it. Capture? Kidnap? I'm a little conflicted about how I can categorize what we're about to do. The other girls say you can't kidnap vanai, they don't count them as human. They aren't really, but they're not animals either. They're part of us after all. I can't help but think (despite what the council would like us to think about them) that if they share any traits with us at all then they at least have to be as sentient as we are.

I wouldn't know. I've never actually seen a full-blooded vanai in the flesh. Yes, having vanai blood means that they shouldn't have anything I don't, but I'm part of the in-between generation. Meaning that my father was human, and by all accounts my family was human. My grandfather was vanai but I only know this, I've never seen him. He's kept with all the other captured vanai inside the city pens, if he's even still alive. My mother– being exactly half– was allowed to mate whomever she wanted. Which was great for my parents, but it means that the responsibility falls on me and my friends to renew the bloodline. Every other generation has to be at least half vanai. That's the rule. It ensures that future halflings have enough vanai blood to keep everyone safe. I've known this would be my destiny all my life. I'm ready. That doesn't make it any less nerve-wracking.

I don't see it, but I can sense it in the others as well. Not the boys though. The two of them ride at the front, waving and blowing kisses at all the human girls and generally lavishing up the attention. As usual. The other girls in our party ignore it and let them indulge. We're all used to it. The boys are all rather spoiled.

Halfling boys are rare, no one is quite sure why. Something about vanai genetics doesn't transfer well through male human genetics. In any case, there's maybe one halfling male for every ten females, so the boys can pretty much get away with murder. Aksha and Baku were the only male halflings in Uthon village, so they've consequently spent their whole lives being doted on. I've personally seen Baku with at least four different human girls in the two weeks we've been in Songak. It doesn't matter, because in the end, he will end up with a vanai mate as well. We all have the same destiny.

The silence is heavy once we're past the gates and the noise of the city disappears behind us. We all ride with our thoughts weighing on our shoulders, our curiosity, and anxiousness. The road slopes upward into the mountains, and the cooler muted colored forests of Songyo surround us and drown out any possibility of anything but what lies ahead for us.

The horses pick up on it as the tension rises the farther we get from the city. Pretty soon they're wickering, flicking their tails nervously, skittering on the road. Aksha and Baku's mounts are the worst. Their air of bravado and lazy confidence is gone, I can see both men sitting up taller, their shoulders tense beneath their ears even from my place at the back of the line. Eventually, Tama gets sick of Baku's horse shying off the road and forces us all to take a break. Tama's always the first to lose patience, so this comes as no surprise.

Her feline eyes are especially harsh as the boys tie up their mounts and fling off their shirts to go running into the nearest stream, disapproval and annoyance dripping from her twisted lips and pinched brow.

"Leave them be," Kessi snickers as she bends down and scoops up a handful of water to splash on her face, "They're just blowing off steam."

Tama's expression doesn't change though, she's not as patient with the boys as everyone else. Probably because one of them is her twin.

Yiren has a map unrolled on her lap, crunching on a rice cracker, "We should reach base camp by evening. According to the council records the wild ones use these hunting trails here that run west of their settlement," She points down at what looks to me to be a formless set of squiggles on the map, "We should be able to intercept them when they come through this pass tomorrow night."

As she talks crumbs from her rice cracker fall onto the maps and then sprinkle down over her skirt. I watch Tama's disapproving expression move from the boys to Yiren, one of her sharp black brows arched over her fierce eyes.

Tama always reminded me of a tigress, beautiful in a scary sort of way.

"Don't speak with your mouth full." She scolds Yiren, who blinks and then looks down at her rice cracker, frowning.

Beside her, Sarissa giggles and helps herself to one of the rice crackers in Yiren's bag, "Lighten up Tama-oi." She grins, adding the honorific on purpose, I suspect, to remind Tama that she is the same age as us and doesn't need to mother us. Even though she will anyway. Tama just likes to be in charge.

Tama's face doesn't soften, but her eyes lose a bit of their sharpness as Sarissa leans in to tap a blushing Yiren on the nose and kiss her softly on the cheek.

"Just think," Kessi says as she climbs back up the bank and smiles at Tama, "By tomorrow you might have someone you can finally order around, and they'll have no choice but to listen."

Tama tips her head to one side, sleek black ponytail brushing her bare shoulders, "Don't be flippant. Purebloods are nothing to joke about. If all of you don't start taking this seriously you're going to end up hurt. These aren't the soft-brained humans that will crawl willing into your bed and get down on their hands and knees to worship your feet. Wild males are dangerous."

"No one's being dismissive of that, Tama," Renyi says serenely, the wiry hunter is perched cross-legged on a boulder, slowly sharpening the blade of her knife, not even looking up as she speaks, "They're joking and playing to dispel anxiety. It's a coping mechanism. Just like your spiky attitude and overbearing bullishness is worse because you're worried about them."

Straight to the core, as usual. We all exchange wry looks as Renyi continues about her weapons maintenance like she didn't just psycho-analyze every single one of us in one stroke.

"Aw, worried about our well-being baby sis?" Baku throws an arm over Tama's shoulders, still dripping water from the creek. Tama curls her lips back as she looks from his arm on her shoulder, to the water he's soaking into her shawl, and promptly slaps him.

Baku and Ashka howl with laughter as Tama spits out a stream of curses in a heavy Uthon dialect. This brings an end to our break, and everyone is back on the horses within minutes, lest we incur more of Tama's wrath.

I fall back to my usual position heading up the rear, and we ride for a few minutes when I notice Aksha has also dropped back. He slips me a secretive smile when I catch his eye, and I am immediately curious even before he speaks.

"Need company?" he asks.

I smile at him lightly but shake my head, "I'm okay, I like it back here, I can keep an eye out for anything sneaking up on us."

Not unlikely out here, and a safety measure I'm used to. At the moment though, I'm distracted by Aksha's attention. He has a softer, more boyish look than Baku, and is a little more laid back. He's usually happy to follow on Baku's heels when it comes to stirring up trouble or getting a rise out of Tama.

"Well if you do get lonely tonight, I could use some company," He says bluntly, adding a touch of warmth to the invitation with a crinkle of soft brown eyes.

I stare at him. Not because I'm insulted, but Aksha has never invited me to his bed before. It was not out of the question. With so few halfling males around, the few that we have inevitably end up being shared. Even for those of us who can find enjoyment in human males, my grandmother once warned me that being with a vanai male would ruin humans for me. It can never be the same, she said, because halflings and vanai understand and complete each other intimately in a way humans can never match up to. It follows that once the vanai have served their purpose of creating halfling children and are returned to the pen, most of the adult halflings are only interested in bedding each other. Even after they've been mated.

I might have been with Aksha eventually, but for a long time now– outside of his human lovers– he's been heavily favored by Tama and Renyi exclusively. The two of them switched off with what seemed like ease, alternating Aksha's attention between them. With Tama being one half of the duo, there seemed little room for any other halfling in Aksha's intimate circle. The rest of us tended to keep our distance. I have never been with a human, and I am plenty used to sharing Baku with the others, though I'm fairly certain I had him first. His family and mine have always lived the closest, and the other girls said this was why Tama seemed to be the most tolerant of me. I'd never considered that tolerance might extend to sharing her lover.

I dart a look ahead on instinct, Tama does glance back to see where Aksha's wandered, but she doesn't look the least bit bothered that he's decided to cozy up to me. And he is riding close, our legs are nearly bumping with each jostle of the horses.

It unsettles me though. While what we're about to do tomorrow might be temporary, it still seems rather cold to spend the night before I meet my mate rolling around with a different man.

"I shouldn't," I tell him, softening the refusal with a guilty smile, "I want to save my energy for the hunt tomorrow."

Aksha shrugs, unaffected, "The offer stands, once this is done. You need only ask."

I lift one brow and tip my chin at him, "Bored of the city girls already?"

Aksha winks at me, grinning, "I like my girls with fangs." He flashes his, two long white incisors, wicked sharp, that he makes descend just for the purpose of showing off before he spurs his horse to catch up with Baku. Leaving me laughing.

It is full dark when we finally glimpse the vanai settlement. We spot it through the breaks in the trees, several hills over from the ridge we stand upon. The lights twinkle in the dark, but the only reason we know it is the vanai settlement is because it's in the place marked for it on the map. Otherwise, from a distance, it looks no different than any other city.

We make camp, and shortly after dinner everyone starts unpacking bedrolls and settling for sleep. I don't think any of us will actually sleep tonight. I can hear tossing and turning all over camp, low male voices that sound like Aksha and Baku talking quietly from their bedrolls. I stare up at the stars and let my mind wander a bit, just imagining.

"Rin?" Yerena, in the bedroll next to mine, turns over and blinks long-lashed pretty round eyes at me.

"Mm?" I answer, because she knows I'm not asleep yet.

"Are you nervous, about tomorrow?"

I want to say that *of course I'm nervous*, everyone is, but I think she probably just wants to talk.

"I don't know. I don't think we can help it, but all halflings do this. I guess there's probably no reason to be."

She sits up a little, threading a strand of dark hair between her fingers, "What do you think you want him to be like, your mate?"

I frown at that, "I don't know that they can be like anything. Except vanai."

Do vanai have specific features we can choose between? My choices in partners were limited, though good. I can fairly confidently say that both Baku and Aksha are objectively attractive, but all halflings are, and from what I've been told, so are vanai.

"Yea but, what would make you pick one over the other?"

I shake my head, "I don't know, I guess I'll know it when I see it."

There's every chance that none of us will find a mate tomorrow. The hunt is mostly ceremony, if we don't get a mate tomorrow we can pick from any of the captive vanai brought in by the traders at the pen in Songak. We do get the choice, so really, maybe I should have given more thought about what specifically, I want for the father of my children. What would make me choose him? It just seemed unnecessary until now, like when I saw him I would just...know. Now of course that sounds ridiculous.

"Do you think maybe it's possible to...I don't know, tame them?"

I jerk my head to gape at her, "Whatever for?"

Yerena shrugs, "I just thought it would be nice. To be able to keep your mate."

"*Keep* them?" I squeak, aghast, "Yerena. We're talking about vanai here. Wild vanai. They're not pets, they're not even human. It's only because of vanai blood that we can even survive the mating, and you think we could *live* with them?"

"No, well, I just...always wondered you know? What if they can be reasoned with and no one's ever tried?"

I know the expression on my face must be flabbergasted because Yerena blushes.

"I'm sure someone's tried," I say, but once I say it, I'm not sure. I've never heard of anyone trying to keep their vanai mates before. I know how vicious and aggressive they are. I know humans don't survive mating full-blooded vanai and that the first halflings were made by very careful planning and a lot of intervention. At the same time, I don't actually *know*, and even now it's hard for me to imagine that a species that looks so much like us possesses no amount of human self-control or reasoning.

"You're probably right." Yerena agrees, and sighs, "I just thought, for a moment, how nice it might be to have a male that was just mine, you know?"

That thought rattles me. It was something that I never considered before because it was mostly impossible for my generation. Yerena is asleep within minutes, but I lay awake, mind spinning. Wondering things that I've never bothered wondering about before.

We find the trail early the next morning and set up lookouts in the brush to wait for the vanai hunting party. The scouts from Songak keep close tabs on all vanai movement in this part of the region, and we know from their observations that the vanai send out their hunting parties every new moon, almost always made up of younger males and a few of the seasoned elders. Rarely does anyone see the female vanai outside the walls of their settlements, which is a good thing, because females are immeasurably more aggressive.

We lie in wait for hours, silent while we hide down in the brush and nibble nervously on snacks. Ividian spots them first from her higher lookout spot at the top of a pine tree and calls down to us. Everyone rushes to get a first look at them as they come into view through the trees and a bubble of nervous excitement wells up inside of me.

My first impression of the wild vanai, is that they don't look very wild at all. They appear at first to be just a normal hunting party, riding in on sturdy-looking mounts, clothed in dark-colored robes and outfitted with an assortment of weaponry. As they draw closer on the trail below our lookout, I can see the more noticeable differences that definitely mark them out as *other*. They're bigger than humans for one, but watching them I can also make out the very distinctly inhuman grace and fluidity in their movements. We follow silently as they move along the trail, settling again when they break at the nearest stream. Everyone's eyes scan the group of hunters, searching. There are about twenty of them, all male, and as we expected most seem to be younger males with three or four of what appear to be elders. I guess, because the elders don't look older in physical appearance, they just seem more relaxed, surer of themselves, and less boisterous than the younglings.

We wait, everyone watching silently. We won't move until someone singles one out, but minutes pass and no one speaks out. I scan the faces of the vanai, waiting for my spark of interest. They are all ethereal actually, with wilder, harsher beauty than human males. Any one of them would make a fine mate, but I don't feel that pull that I expected. Being around halflings my whole life has made me somewhat jaded when it comes to beautiful beings, and the fact that the vanai are all quite attractive is not as impressive as it might be to a human. The others must think the same, because a quick glance at the other girls shows me everyone is examining the vanai with the same sort of unimpressed detachment. I'm starting to think we will end up leaving without a single one of us picking a mate, when I notice movement by the bank.

A younger male becomes visible among a group of his companions, one I hadn't noticed as the group was moving. I sit up a little, something about this particular young male catching my attention. He's rifling through the bags with a couple of his companions, but when he stands I notice he's several inches taller than the others.

That isn't what captures my attention though. It's when one of his peers makes a remark, and all of them laugh and grin. I notice the smile on his face, the way it makes his eyes light up, and that his disarming smile is bracketed by a very human set of dimples.

I don't think over it much when the words are out of my mouth, "That one. I want that one." I declare, pointing at the young male with the dimples.

The other girls glance from me to the young male on the bank, Tama is already getting to her feet, gripping the hilt of her sword at her side. She looks left to her twin, and Baku nods at her and wordlessly both of our males start to move.

No one asks me if I'm sure, no one questions what prompted my choice or why I sound so sure. Everyone just moves.

"We'll push them into the woods. Baku and Aksha will get him cut off from the rest of the group. Rin, you take the long way around and make your move from there." I meet Tama's eyes as she delivers the instructions. She wants to make sure I understand, and I do. Once he's cut off from the group I am on my own, I have to capture him on my alone. That's tradition.

Sarissa elbows me as she gets to her feet, "You have the serum?" She asks in a low voice.

I reach a hand into the pouch at my waist, closing my fingers around the cool glass of the syringe with the paralyzing serum, and nod in reassurance. We scatter, and I scramble down the hill and find my horse, vaulting into the saddle and taking the reins just as the first shouts of surprise and defiance echo from the streambed.

I ride through the underbrush, my smaller, stockier mare makes quick works of the uneven and often tricky terrain and I make it to the main road and ride in the direction of the stream. I can hear bits and pieces of the confrontation, but my attention zeroes in on the subtler sounds coming from the forest ahead. I make it to the midway point just as the other horse appears on the other end of the road.

The young man I singled out on the stream bed rides up on a much larger bay stallion, looking noticeably more ruffled and a whole lot more confused. He's looking over his shoulder and at the road around him, trying to get his bearings. I can tell Baku and Aksha have given him a good go of it by the small cut I spot across a jutting cheekbone.

He stops his mount abruptly with a jerk of the reins when he sees me waiting for him. We're several paces apart, but we're close enough that I can make out more details than when I was watching him from above. He's even more striking up close, all smooth cut angles and fine bones. His eyes are deep set and angular, but a warm earthy brown. His shoulders are broader up close, and he's much larger in person. Twice my size nearly, even if I wasn't the smallest halfling among my peers. He's in cotton robes of dark blue, but I can see the finely made pommel of the sword strapped to his waist.

He eyes me in the same careful way and I can hear him clearly when he says between breathes, "Halfling."

He says it in vanai, but the language translates easily without my conscious intent to do so. The language is as much a part of my blood as the instinct to flash my fangs and growl at him. I unsheathe my sword and grip my reins, and I see the slight stiffening of him bracing himself just before I spur my mare forward and come at him. For all that he looks ready for a fight, I notice that he does nothing but block me when I rush him. I wheel my mare and move to strike, and he raises his blade and makes a grunt of effort when the blades clang together, but he doesn't move to retaliate. His mount backs up and mine gains ground, and steel rings as I swing, again and again, trying to throw him off balance.

It's a task for sure, he's a large male, strong and solid. I can feel it each time he lifts his sword to block me. But the more I swing the more confused I get. I can see he's more than capable of wielding the weapon, but he does nothing more than block my swings and push back. He makes no move to strike at me, even while I can see the toll the effort is taking on him by the rise and fall of his chest and the flex of his jaw.

Frustration fueling my strength, I use one of Baku's favorite moves, underhand my sword, and swing up in one and the new move finally does the trick. He tips off balance and I can see him twisting his torso and expertly rolling into the fall as he tumbles from his horse. I jump down to follow him, and by the time I dismount he's already back on his feet, sword at the ready.

I blink at his appearance. Raven black bangs slide over his brow and shade his striking eyes, but he keeps his gaze trained on my every move. His hair is cut short, which is unusual, every halfling I know keeps theirs long and I just assumed vanai would be the same. His feet are spread, stance braced. He moves fast and with grace and visible experience, and yet, even now face to face, he doesn't move to strike me.

I frown, watching him, waiting. He's breathing hard and I can see the fast calculation in his eyes, but his body doesn't move from its protective stance. *Why isn't he attacking?*

I slash at him, and he parries again, but does nothing more than bat my blade away and back up another step. No movement forward. *What on earth?* The way he watches me looks almost anxious; he should be fighting back. He's more than capable of it, I can see he can, so why isn't he moving? I don't have time to wonder, If I don't get him down then his companions might have time to come for him, so I go in again and again. No retaliation, but he's tiring. This is his second fight and only my first, I have more energy to expend and he's using more of his to hold me off.

He knows it as much as I do, I can see it on his face. A bit of his frustration breaks through when he is forced to block a particularly vicious set of strikes and his lips curl back and I get a good close view of his bared fangs. And holy gods, his *fangs*. His are several inches long, deadly sharp, and so large that they curl down over his bottom row of teeth. They make halfling fangs look like baby teeth.

It startles me a little and he gets a few seconds of reprieve. Without meaning to I feel *my* fangs descend, and he sees them when he glances up and eyes my clenched teeth. He lets out a small laugh, but it's enough to incense me. This time, I get in under his guard, he grunts in dismay as his sword is knocked from his hand and goes stock still as I press my blade to his throat.

I'm panting as hard as he is, and I see the flicker in his eyes when he looks down at my smile and my much tinier fangs. It doesn't dampen my victorious shine though.

"Gotcha," I breathe. He looks resigned, watching my face and then closing his eyes, waiting for the final strike. It doesn't come from my blade, and he lets out a yelp of surprise when in two fast movements I pull the syringe out of my pouch and stick it into the closest patch of skin I can find on him, which happens to be his neck. He jerks back, just avoiding the blade, pulling the empty syringe from the juncture of his neck and staring at me in bewilderment. I watch with bemused curiosity as his eyes roll up into his head and he slumps backward, making a rather large thump as his body goes limp.

I wait a few minutes to make sure the paralytic is fully distributed, and then I step forward to examine him. He's so much larger up close, and a bit of unease trickles through me. How am I supposed to mate with him? He could easily crush me without even meaning to. Then, of course, I do have vanai blood, so I am theoretically harder to break. Not that I feel the need to test out the theory.

This unease is replaced with something even more unsettling as I crouch down beside his head. I push the black bangs off his brow, ignoring the slight dampness of his skin from the fight. I suck in a breath as I get my clearest look at him, his features relaxed by unconsciousness. Like this, he is less threatening, and without the imminent danger of being bitten, I see him clearer. And he looks so young. Very young.

A hard ball of guilt settles into my stomach as I look him over. He's clearly a full-grown adult, filled out and comfortable in his body, strong and hardened with muscle, but he's a very *young* adult. It's hard to tell because vanai age slowly, slowing even more when they reach twenty-five before they stop aging altogether somewhere around age thirty. But this young man hasn't reached even the midpoint yet. I assure myself that he can't be a teenager, he's much too filled out. But he can be anywhere from twenty to twenty-five.

And now he's going to spend the rest of his very long life in captivity, because of me. I chew on my bottom lip, try to convince myself that this is necessary. We need more halflings, if it wasn't him, it would have been someone else. Looking for some kind of proof, some reassurance that I have reason to be putting this male that may or not be even younger than me in chains, I push gently at his lips, also trying to ignore how soft and very plush they feel. His fangs have retracted, but I can still see them nestled in his top row of teeth. The sharpened points of the incisors still jut down, large and noticeable. I touch the tip of one and yank my hand back, hissing and staring down at my fingertip where a small bead of blood is already welling from the nick. His fangs were sharp enough to cut me with that small of a touch. They're lethal. And paired with his size and inhuman speed...

He's a killer. I remind myself, if not now then he would be eventually. Immortal and ruthless. Yet when I lean back and examine him, the thought enters my mind that he didn't attack me. Up close, I can't see any distinction between this full-blooded vanai and the halflings I know. We look the same. His skin is a bit lighter than mine from his northern blood, and he's much larger than my males, his fangs more deadly. But there are no other physical distinctions. Anyone could tell he's not human, his features are much harsher and his eyes have a slightly sharper shape, but side by side with a male halfling, I don't think I could accurately guess which one was half-blood and which was pure blood.

He could obviously tell, but his sense of smell is also more enhanced than mine. We look like the same species to the naked eye.

My musings are interrupted by the sound of horses. The other halflings ride up the road toward us as I stand. Tama dismounts first, Aksha and Baku and Renyi join her, inspecting my catch. Renyi pats me on the back and the others exchange congratulations with me as the girls examine the young vanai male.

"Let's get the cuffs on him and get on the road," Tama instructs, and Sarissa is already bringing the cuffs as Aksha and Baku prop up the unconscious vanai and get his arms behind his back.

"What did you do with the other wild ones?" I ask her as the boys lift my new mate onto an extra horse, setting him face down over the saddle.

Tama gives me a guarded look as she climbs up onto her horse, "We let them go. You will be the only one returning with a mate this time."

My brow creases from the odd note in her voice and the closed-off expression on her face. Something is off about her statement, but I can't puzzle it out. She turns away and I make my way back to my mare, I double back to go and collect the vanai's stallion. No need to waste a good horse, and I tie him to the back of my saddle before I ride on to join the others and usher my prize toward home.

Chapter Two

Our return echoes off the city walls as we approach Songak, and by the time we're through the gates the citizens have come out to welcome us with much fanfare. Once they spot my catch, the cheering turns to jeers and rather mean-spirited gestures in regards to the vanai. The vehemence becomes strong enough that I ride a little closer, tensing with the concern that the humans might start to throw things or make moves to harm my would-be mate. I'm not honestly sure what the purpose of the jeering is. He's out cold so it's not like he can hear them, but then I guess maybe this is their outlet and a way to vent their despise of the vanai. A balm if you will, and some retribution for all the humans stolen and killed by his wild counterparts. I still ready myself in case someone decides to be bold. I understand their hatred for his kind, but I'm going to need him in his best condition, and it's not exactly fair when he's not even awake to defend himself.

The others break off to head home, or at least what they've been calling home since relocating to Songak. Tama stays with me and we take the young vanai to the confinement unit. I watch as the human caretakers unload him and a small group of human women pull him into exam to be looked over by their doctor and cleaned up for presentation. My stuff is gathered and brought to confinement for me, and I briefly go up after bidding Tama goodbye to check the small apartment that will be my temporary living space for the next few weeks.

When one of the caretakers comes to tell me he's ready I head down the stairs to the secured space beneath my apartment. The door is sealed with several locks on the outside and only opens with a specific combination. Inside, the room is small with nothing but a barred window for light. The floors are padded, and a shower and repository are built into a lowered tiled area in one corner. The only piece of furniture is a large bed. No sheets or blankets. And in the very center of the room in another cushioned seating area, my vanai capture has been left propped against the bench, head lolling back.

They've stripped him of his clothing, which is no surprise, and added a metal collar and wrist and ankle cuffs that attach to a mechanism in the floor and a winch that can shorten or lengthen the chains using the control panel on the wall behind me. The chains can also be moved around the room by the same mechanism, for ease of mobility.

They've given him the dignity of a blanket over his lap, but the rest of his body is left bare for my perusal. In the well-lit space, I get an eyeful of hard lines of muscle beneath lightly tanned skin. He's a beautiful creature, even if vicious.

My attention turns to the tray by the door and the assortment of serums, syringes, and devices I've been left. I identify the counter-mixture to the paralytic and pick it up to approach him. I'm careful as I step up and crouch down beside him. He's been bathed and I can smell the soap on his skin, his black bangs are still partially damp where they hang down over his forehead. Someone has applied an ointment over the small cut across his cheekbone. He was very carefully readied for me, a thought that stirs a fire in my gut. I reach down and turn his shackled wrist, my fingers tingling where they touch his warm skin. I find a vein and insert the syringe and then back up until my shoulders touch the wall. I get comfortable on the bench beside the now securely locked door and reach up to keep one hand on the control panel of the chains while I wait.

It doesn't take long; within minutes I see his fingers twitch and his limbs start to move. It takes the longest for him to pick his head up, blearily open his stunning eyes, and with a wary look, he examines the room. Then his gaze pivots toward me. My hand closes on the control lever, bracing myself, preparing for the minute he realizes what has happened and he springs up, snarling, clawing, ready to tear me apart with his bare hands. It never comes.

He stares at me for a few seconds, and I see the reality of his situation slowly dawn on him. He doesn't explode into motion; he doesn't even look angry or surprised. He simply tips his head to one side and looks me up and down with serene brown eyes. The first thing he says isn't "where am I?" or "what is going on?"

Instead, his brows draw together as he stares at me and states, plainly, "You're not a northerner." Factual and placid. Observational.

I blink several times and frown at him, "I...well, I mean no. I'm not."

The words come out in Vanai, a language that I've never spoken until today, and yet it slides off my tongue naturally. Without thinking. I've never heard the words I'm speaking before, yet they're as natural as breathing.

He's still staring at me, curious gaze tracking over my form. I look down and realize why he's drawn this immediate conclusion about my origins. I'm wearing a soft cotton shawl that leaves my shoulders and midriff bare, a wrap skirt, and bangles on my upper arms. Even my feet are bare. It's southern-style clothing. We do and have worn the heavier northern silk blouses and full heavy skirts, but it's summer in Songyo now and southern clothing keeps us a lot cooler in this weather, so most of the halflings from Uthon have opted to wear our traditional outfits.

"You're darker too," He notes, again, factual.

I open and close my mouth, "I...well I'm from the south. From Uthon, twelve of us came here from Uthon."

He looks at me curiously, those perceptive eyes wandering my face, "Aren't there cities in the south?"

His voice is a low, clear tenor. It's conversational, and the juxtaposition of his lovely voice and calm demeanor, while he's sitting there naked in chains, has me a little off-kilter.

"Um, the halflings in Songak needed reinforcements. The lower birthrate in the past few years has left the younger generation unbalanced so they offered to relocate small groups of us from the south up here."

Why am I explaining this to him?

He nods calmly, seeming to absorb this without much confusion. Then to my great surprise, he looks at me expectantly and raises his brows.

"So what's next?"

I blink at him, "What?"

He spreads his hands, the chains attached to his wrists clinking, "I expect you have to do something with me. This doesn't look like a cage or a prison cell after all. I'm guessing I'm not going to be executed anytime soon."

His nonchalance is throwing me off, completely.

"Why are you so calm about this?" I ask him, since he seems open to conversation, "Why aren't you trying to fight or break through the chains or kill me?"

He snorts out a laugh, the points of his fangs flashing and those dimples appearing around his mouth, "Break through the chains? That'd be a waste of time and energy. I'm sure your people wouldn't have gone through the effort of outfitting a place like this without at least making sure the chains were vanai-proof. And what would I want to kill you for?"

I stumble over a response to that and he notices.

"Not what you expected?" he guesses, "Thought you'd be dealing with a crazed blood-thirsty monster incapable of rationale or reason?"

That's exactly what I thought I'd be dealing with. And the fact that he's not like that and is sitting there perfectly calmly, conversing as normally and as logically as I would with any of my males, is giving me a small bit of distress.

"You're far more lucid than I expected," I admit, then I narrow my eyes at him because even a halfling, in the same situation, would at least be a little alarmed by being held captive, "You act as if you know exactly what's going to happen."

His mouth tips up at one corner, amused, I think. Which is even more startling.

"You think vanai don't know what happens when our people go missing? You honestly think that your kind could steal our younglings for generation after generation and no one would realize what was happening?" He shakes his head, "We know. And we realize it's always a possibility that we end up in this exact situation whenever we leave the walls of Hwa-mungung."

I fumble mentally over hearing the name of the vanai city for the first time, gaping at him. It is believed that the reason the vanai never retaliate when their kind is captured or killed is that they are generally solitary creatures that operate with single-minded self-preservation. That was believable until I saw the air of camaraderie shared between this male and his companions on the bank, the easy and familiar way they were with each other. Even between the older and younger males. It's clear that they were quite close with one another, and had been there as a group.

"Then why don't you–"

"Try to get them back?" he finishes, he gazes at me for a moment, seemingly considering how to answer, his lips twist with what looks like confliction.

"The answer probably wouldn't make sense to you, judging by how little you seem to know of our kind."

I scowl, he said it with the clear intention of including me in the category of "our kind" and I resent being classified as the same species as vanai. He recognizes my displeasure immediately and barks out a laugh.

"Don't like being called vanai? Yet you've brought me here to add more vanai blood to your line," He says smugly, smirking through the point of his fangs.

"It's a necessity." I retort, I can feel my brow crinkling as a result of both my indignation at his amusement and my confusion.

He makes a small shrugging motion, like it doesn't matter to him either way. He seems so...normal. It occurs to me that if I saw him on the street, I'd never be able to tell he was a pureblood. I have a lot of questions, most of them occurring simultaneously. The most pressing seems to be obvious, but it also never occurred to me to ask such a thing.

"Do you have a name?" I wonder. I don't know if vanai have such benign things as names. I never thought they were capable of being human enough to even address each other.

He seems to find that funny, his eyes crinkling at the corner.

"Yes, I have a name. My parents gave me a name at birth, the same way yours did. It's Ryu."

I can't explain why, but suddenly having a name to match his face makes this whole thing seem that much more real. He's an actual being, with a personality, a name, memories, feelings. He's no longer the faceless monster I once imagined I would be facing when this day came.

His gaze tracks my expression, reading the thoughts right as they cross my face.

"Does it make you uncomfortable to know I have something as normal as a name?" he prods, and it does make me uncomfortable. Even more so that he seems to understand my emotions.

"I just, I sort of thought vanai would have no need for something as human as names," I admit, not without a small bit of heat flooding my cheeks.

"Hm," He grunts, and I notice one of his brows tick up, but he doesn't comment on it further, "And what should I call you, now that we're getting familiar?" he asks.

I debate answering, but there's no guideline on how to do this. I don't know if anyone ever even bothers to talk to the vanai before they mate them. I've never heard anyone mention names before. What harm could him knowing who I am do though? It's not as if the information will be of any use to him.

"Rin," I say, letting out a breath.

He passes me a thoughtful look, brown eyes full of depth that I am totally unprepared for.

"That flows well," He comments, "Rin and Ryu."

I can only stare at him.

"Well," he rolls his shoulders back with apparent ease, "Better get on with it. What are you supposed to do now?" he prompts.

I hesitate but then pick up the syringe filled with amber-gold liquid and hold it up so he can see it.

"I need to give you this," I tell him.

One of his finely groomed brows lifts with skepticism, "And what is in that?"

I chew on my lip, reluctant about the wisdom of telling him, but he's watching me, and clearly willing to wait for an answer.

"It's the breeding drug. It will, as I understand, trigger your instinct to mate."

It is a safety measure, a strong one. I don't tell him more because I also know that the drug basically makes them feverish with lust until it is the only thing they can think about. It eliminates a lot of the danger of mating with them because the need to mate overrides the urge to attack or injure. It incapacitates as well as makes them willing to complete the union. It is required, but from what I understand it's also not pleasant for the vanai involved because if the urge is not relieved it can be quite painful.

Ryu seems to guess that there is more to it anyway, I can see his jaw clenching and the wary look that enters his eyes.

"It is required. If I don't give it to you then the caretakers will just come in later and give it to you anyway. We have to try and conceive at least once a day if not more, for the next month."

This makes his brows shoot up, "Your people seem to have a lot of faith in vanai virility."

I grip the syringe, "I think it will be easier on you if I'm the one who gives you the drug. The humans here are not fond of vanai, and they won't be gentle. Will you cooperate?"

He cocks his head at me, "Are you asking my permission to drug me?" his lips twitch with humor.

I can feel my cheeks heating again, "You have not been aggressive or threatening toward me yet and you seem like you can be reasoned with. So I'd prefer to not have to force this, for both of our sakes."

He considers this with a small, slightly bemused smile and finally nods, "I will cooperate."

I blow out a small breath of relief and turn toward the control panel, I stop with one hand on the levers and look over my shoulder, "I have to restrain your arms behind your back and shorten the chains a little, for my safety. It's just procedure."

Ryu doesn't seem bothered by this, he simply shrugs and nods once at me, "As you will."

I pull down on the lever and gears crank as the chains fastened to his wrists pull taut and his arms are slowly pulled back behind him. The chains around his ankles tighten as well and I wait until all the machinery stops clanking before I approach. Ryu holds still as I cross the room, though he sits up and watches me, he doesn't pull at or resist the chains and he doesn't move away when I bend down beside him and uncap the syringe.

I dart a look at his face as I press my fingers to the bare skin on his arm, and quickly pierce the skin with the needle, pushing down on the plunger. The skin around his eyes tightens a bit but otherwise, he doesn't react.

"Sorry," I mutter and without really thinking about it I rub the injection site lightly before pulling back and standing up. I have to keep the chains taut until the drug is in effect so I only step back a few paces and look down at Ryu's expression. A nagging thought digs at me as I meet his bright-eyed gaze.

"How old are you?" I ask him.

Ryu shivers involuntarily, the first sign the drug is starting to take effect, but he shakes it off and holds my gaze.

"I was born in the year of the rabbit. This is my second cycle."

Twenty-four. He is twenty-four. And that hard ball of guilt is back, pressing against the inside of my ribs. I wince and Ryu sees it.

"Oh, we're not the same age then? Interesting." He squints at me, "Are you...older? Younger?"

I grind my teeth together but think I should probably tell him, "I was born in the year of the tiger. Same cycle."

A wide grin splits his face, "Ah, well then, *Nooe.*"

He bows his head respectfully and my brain immediately translates the vanai honorific to *older sister*.

I blow out a breath. It's not a huge difference, only a year, but he *is* younger than me, and now it is very difficult to look at him as nothing but an emotionless monster. Not with that spark in his eyes, those boyish dimples framing his mouth, or that playful grin on his lips. My stomach flips, and I cross the room to wait, watching him for changes while battling the inner turmoil that thinking of him as an individual is causing me.

Ryu stops talking as the drug starts to make its way through his system and I can visibly see him beginning to fight the effects. It begins subtle, I notice he's breathing a bit faster, and his eyes have started to look a little glazed. A little while later he drops his head, like he no longer has the energy to hold it up, and the curtain of his bangs blocks most of his expression, but I can see the tightening of his shoulders. The veins start to stand out in his neck as he clenches and unclenches his jaw.

His whole body looks as if it draws up taut like a bowstring ready to snap.

He's fully in the throes of it by the time I start to feel true concern. I knew roughly what the drug would do, but watching it work its way through a real person is a different experience. I take a few cautious steps toward him, my own body humming with tension as I realize his shoulders are now trembling slightly and at some point, he's become feverish and as I get closer I can see his bangs are now slick with sweat. I can hear his breathing has worsened, turning into ragged, shuddery pants that make his shoulders heave with each burst of air.

"Are you okay?" I ask quietly, which is a stupid question of course because I can see that he's not.

Ryu inhales sharply, apparently not having noticed me approaching until that point. His spine goes rigid and when he speaks his voice comes out in a rough rasp.

"Managing," He croaks out.

"When it gets to be too much just let me know and..."

"Let me," He cuts me off, and it sounds more like a growl than words, "Let me adjust. I have to get some control back or I'll..."

He trails off, but I get the gist. I scuttle back until I get to the wall and fiddle with my hands nervously while I wait. I'd like to get it over with, but clearly, Ryu thinks it's not safe yet, and he would know better than I would. Minutes pass, in total it takes close to an hour before Ryu's a trembling mess, huddled forward, all of the visible muscles in his body straining. I can see the sweat trickling down his neck and he's panting loudly now, struggling with each inhale.

I get up again, moving slowly so I don't startle him. I bend to try and get a good look at his face, but I can't see anything with his head bowed as it is.

"Ryu?" I start cautiously, now even more unsure of what to expect. I didn't think even with the warnings, that the drug would be quite this...intense.

I jump when Ryu's voice comes out, two octaves deeper than his normal voice, scratchy and vibrating with an almost animalistic timbre.

"Please," He rasps, and I gasp when he lifts his head to look at me. I can't help it, his eyes...the previously light brown irises are now *glowing,* illuminated as if from behind by an amber-gold light. And his fangs are fully descended now and bared, the sharp ends glinting in the light as he speaks, pleads more like.

"Hurts. Can't wait anymore."

I blanch at that; I think about what he said and my eyes drop automatically to his lap and...oh. Yes, he's sporting a very large and very visible erection. My mouth goes dry, but the space between my thighs goes very wet. Ryu's nostrils flare, and I flush as I realize he can probably smell it.

This is confirmed when he lets out a very low and emanating growl, and my thighs wobble in anticipation, my body reacting without my consent to the sound of his male arousal.

"Okay," I whisper, because even though his eyes and his bared fangs are terrifying, I'm also intensely curious and a very non-human part of me is thrumming with excitement. I take a step back, keeping my eyes on him as I reach back for the control panel.

"I'm going to release the tension on your arms and legs, so you can move."

Ryu nods, his glowing eyes meet mine and a shiver runs down my spine, "Don't be scared, I'm going to be a little rougher than I'd like and it might be intense at first, but I can't hurt you. Just don't fight me."

I let out a shuddery breath, my hands shake, but there's a growing fire in my belly and my fingertips tingle to touch him.

"Just...don't bite me," I say, eyeing his gleaming fangs.

Ryu shoots me a look and laughs humorlessly, "I'm going to have to bite you, if you want my seed to take. No?"

I flush scarlet, feeling foolish. He's right, he has to bite me. Vanai can't conceive children outside of a mating, and to mate me, he has to mark me.

"Oh," I squeak, "Right."

I turn around, grab the lever, look back and catch his gaze. Ryu nods once, encouraging me.

I take a deep breath and then I lower the lever and release the slack on his chains. I don't even see him move. One second Ryu is secure against the seating bench and then the gears crank and the chains go slack and there's a blur of movement and then I'm on the floor, face down and there's a body above me, pressing me into the mats, hips pinning mine and a hard shape between my thighs.

I let a surprised squeal and rough fingers wind through my hair, holding me immobile while another big hand pushes up the hem of my skirt.

"Sorry," Ryu says beside my ear, his voice rumbling in his chest and vibrating against my back. He's breathing a mile a minute and I swear my own heart is thundering to keep up, "I don't think I can be gentle," He warns. I don't think he's exaggerating; his whole body is trembling like he's fighting desperately to keep a hold of his self-control.

"It's okay," I tell him, because I am ready for this. I am, and I make my body go limp beneath him, accepting.

Ryu buries his nose in my neck, inhaling, letting out a pained groan of desire. His hips roll into mine from behind and I feel the length of him rubbing against my thighs. Heat punches through my gut and liquid dribbles between my thighs, slickening, reacting to his dominating hold and obvious desire.

His lips are hot on my neck, and I bite back a moan as his tongue licks up the column of my throat. My skin prickles as the hand at my skirt pushes it up and cold air brushes my thighs and my bare ass. Ryu's fingers dig into my hip bone as he pushes my thighs apart with his knees and nestles in between. He's placing small kisses over my shoulder in warning, in placation as he pushes his hips up. My body arches, and I think I'm ready, but the minute I feel the head of his cock breaching my folds everything inside of me melts to a molten core.

I whimper as he pushes inside, impaling himself in one smooth sheath. Ryu freezes for a second and then snarls against my skin. Goosebumps race up my spine and more heat spills between my legs, aiding him as he begins to shuttle. He plunges in until the front of his pelvis is flush with my backside, and the sheer size of him inside of me has me seeing stars and moaning as his fingers tighten in my hair and he slams in with more aggression. He holds on for an admirably long few moments, giving me time to adjust, but then I whimper and my vagina squeezes around him as arousal licks through my center and a vicious snarl rips from him.

His hands become punishing and his movements ruthless. I'm pinned, unable to do anything but plead wordlessly for more as he pounds me from behind and I can already feel the bruises forming on my hips. It is not gentle, but it's delicious, and every slam of his hips has my head swirling and lightning sparking across my nerve endings. I can feel it winding through me already, but then Ryu moves his hand, pushing beneath me till he finds the bud of nerves and his fingers close around my clit. I yelp and then buck, pushing him inadvertently deeper. Ryu's fingers play me expertly, and I'm a crying mess as my release builds and builds and then crests. I can feel my channel contracting as I come, sucking him in, closing like a vice.

Ryu's deep, animalistic growl should be frightening, but instead, the sound sends a signal to my brain that has my blood feeling like lit mercury in my veins and every cell in my body responding in kind. Ryu lets go his grip on my hair only to grip my chin and turn me toward him. His mouth is harsh and claiming on mine, and I moan into the kiss as his tongue twists around mine and I eagerly lap up the taste of him. He breathes out and thrusts his hips in deep.

"Get ready," He says against my lips and then pulls back. I understand a second later as his pounding thrusts become more frantic, hurried, and then it comes at the same time. The hot burst of semen, Ryu's wrecked groan of pleasure, and then the abrupt and shocking pierce of his fangs as he sinks them into my shoulder.

I cry out, surprised despite myself, but the sharp pain of the bite is eased a few seconds later by a strange overwhelming warmth that seems to spread through my limbs and relaxes my body into pliance. Ryu holds on until the last spurt of seed, and then I feel his mouth leave my shoulder and I lay flat, stunned by the dull throb of the bite and the brutality of the entire mating. I'm even more shocked that I liked it. More than liked it, I think. My blood still feels like it's on fire and my belly is tight and fluttery, and my pussy is still full of vanai cock and come.

Chapter Three

We don't move for several minutes, but then Ryu slowly withdraws and props himself back up against the bench, giving me space. His eyes are back to their warm brown, though hazy, but his cheeks are flushed with color and he's still panting with effort.

"Did it go away?" I ask him, catching my own breath as I sit up and fix my skirt.

He nods once but lifts a shackled hand to motion me forward. I tip my head but scoot toward him across the floor. He holds out his arm and I look up at him in question.

"Bite me. You have to mark me to complete the mating bond, if you don't, we will both be hurting bad in about an hour," He explains.

I jerk in surprise, "Oh."

I wonder briefly why I wasn't instructed to do that in my training, but I grip his wrist lightly and lick my lips, squeezing my eyes shut a little as I force my fangs to descend. Ryu watches me through heavy-lidded eyes as I lower my head and pause slightly over his wrist. I'm a little reluctant because I've never bitten anyone before, but Ryu doesn't look nervous and that helps.

I bite down and feel my fangs pierce the skin and I jump a little at the hot burst of blood and the copper taste that fills my mouth. My apprehension is replaced by pure pleasure as the taste of Ryu's blood settles on my tongue and turns. A completely involuntary moan escapes my throat as the copper taste turns suddenly sweet, rich, and my entire body starts to buzz. It's the strangest thing I've ever felt, warm, and comforting, yet shocking and electric all at once. It doesn't make sense, nor does the sudden burst of possessiveness I feel or the way his blood has stopped tasting like blood and instead tastes like pure chocolate and I can't stop drinking.

I don't remember doing it, I don't even think I move consciously. But when clarity comes back to me I find myself with a solid male body beneath me. I've somehow knocked Ryu flat and I'm now straddling him, my hands tangled in his hair and my mouth fiercely dominating his. I jerk back, stumbling and landing flat on my butt in my haste to get off of him. I'm gasping for breath and Ryu looks just as breathless as he sits up, hair messy and eyes bright amber again.

"Wha- what happened?" I gape, looking around for something to make sense.

"You attacked me," Ryu says with a bemused smirk. He doesn't look at all alarmed by the fact that I just knocked him over and threw myself on top of him.

"I...I didn't mean to–"

"It's alright." Ryu flashes me a sympathetic smile, dimples out, "The mating bond is quite intense, isn't it?"

I place a hand on my chest and slowly exhale to steady myself, "I wasn't warned about that."

Ryu's smirk turns into a frown, "It seems rather careless of them not to warn you beforehand."

I look up at him, "Do both mates always need to be marked to complete the bond?"

Ryu's frown only deepens, "Yes. If the bond is not completed things get uncomfortable fast. It becomes an overwhelming need to fulfill it. That's what that breeding drug earlier did in essence, it imitated what a bite does if left uncompleted, and sped up, obviously."

I chew on the inside of my cheek, thinking. I didn't know that about the bond, and it leaves me with a lot of questions about how my world works. How my family even exists, yet I can feel the evidence of it even now. There's a tightening in my gut, a pull that makes me want to move closer to Ryu. I can feel his touch on me and the urge to touch him. I feel the invisible bond between us like it's as real and solid as the chains around his wrists. Ryu's breath on my cheek startles me out of my musings, he appears to be checking my body.

"Did I hurt you?" he asks, concern creasing his forehead.

I shake my head, "I'm going to have some bruises, and I think if I was fully human I'd probably have some broken bones, you're not light, but my body seems to be built for that."

Ryu grunts, but his eyes still search my skin for any signs of injury, "That was mild for a vanai mating honestly, there's usually a lot more growling and fangs involved. Most of the time newly mated pairs have to be moved into special quarters so they don't destroy things." He lifts his gaze to look around at the padded room, "Well, I suppose that's what this is for."

I laugh, "Yeah, I knew it was going to be rough. But I kind of liked it, I was ready for it anyway."

Ryu's gaze focuses on my face, "I didn't scare you?"

He probably should have, but I can still feel the heat gathering between my thighs as I think about the way he dominated me, "No. But I wasn't expecting the whole glowing eye thing."

Ryu blinks, "Glowing ey- Oh."

His expression turns sheepish, I'm struck by the thought that it's actually kind of cute, "I thought I had that under control. I was trying not to startle you."

"It's normal?" I question.

He grimaces, "Our eyes glow when we...well we call it 'going feral', it basically signifies that one of us is in the throes of a frenzy. Most of the time it also means a total loss of control."

That draws my brows together, "Does that happens often?"

Ryu rubs at his jaw, "Outside of mating, no. It's quite normal and harmless when you're mating, but vanai can go feral if the mating bond is not completed or we're separated from our mate for long. Then it's dangerous to anyone *but* our mate."

I say nothing as I let that thought settle, "Do my eyes do that?" I wonder.

Ryu's lips curve into a grin, "They did just now when you threw yourself at me."

I give him a flat look, not amused by how pleased he seems to be by my loss of control. I notice there's a bit of blood smeared on his lips. His blood. My gaze drops to his wrist and I impulsively reach out, turning his arm so that I can see the two clean puncture marks left behind on the tanned skin. He's still bleeding lightly, and I still taste him on my tongue.

"I've never bitten anyone before," I say out loud, musing.

"Well, I should hope not."

I jerk my head up, Ryu's watching me examine his arm with a creased brow.

"You only bite to mark your mate, I would think– if you plan on my siring your offspring– that you would not already be mated," He elaborates, looking increasingly distressed by my cluelessness.

I stare at him. I feel like I'm missing something. He thinks I should know this, but I didn't. I knew that vanai have to bite someone to mate them, but I don't know why marking someone else would affect his ability to make children with me.

"Would that...complicate things?" I question.

Ryu's looking at me now as if he's genuinely alarmed by my lack of knowledge and my spine straightens instinctively in defense.

"Most of us," He says slowly, "Can only have one mate at a time. The bond is like its own living thing, if you already marked someone else, you very likely would not have enjoyed what we just did at all."

I look down, turning this information over. I rub my thumb over one of the puncture marks on his arm, thinking absently. I don't comment on the way this is news to me, but I cringe at the bite mark when another drop of his blood wells from the wound.

"It looks gruesome," I mutter.

"That was nothing. Like a cat bite."

When I look up he's grinning teasingly at me. I snort.

"You should see yours," He says.

I lift my hand automatically to the back of my shoulder. I'd almost forgotten about it, it doesn't throb anymore, but I can feel the mark of his fangs there. When I drop my arm there's no blood on my hand, so it must've clotted some time ago.

"I'm sure it'll fade," I say calmly. Ryu's eyes narrow again, and I realize I've once again troubled him with my unintentional ignorance when he replies simply.

"No, it won't."

I eye him, curious.

"It is an identifier. The mark won't fade, it's permanent, and so is my scent on you and yours on me. It keeps other vanai away. Yours won't fade on me either."

I let go of his arm, but I can feel the frown on my face. I suddenly feel out of my depth. I know by the easy way he's telling me these things that Ryu is not lying. He has no reason to try and feed me false information, but these are things I really should have known. Why didn't the council tell us? Why do I get the feeling this mating bond is much more serious than we were told it was?

I think of all the halflings before me and the vanai mates locked up inside the pen. They would have known, wouldn't they? Why didn't my grandmother tell me? Surely, the way I'm feeling now, like I need to be touching Ryu, the way that my body seems to keep pulling me toward him, is not unique to our mating.

I stand up, smoothing out my skirt, "I should get us something to eat. It's been hours since you were brought in, you're probably hungry. And thirsty."

I turn toward the door and take two steps before I pause. I spin to look back at Ryu and gasp, he's standing right behind me, and I have to lean back to look up into his face. I didn't hear him move.

Seeing that he's startled me, Ryu makes an apologetic face but he doesn't move away, he's close enough that I can feel the heat on his skin.

"Sorry." He winces, "It's the bond, I..." he rubs at the back of his neck, "It's just instinctual. To follow you, I didn't mean to frighten you."

My fingers twitch, I don't understand why I feel the impulse to comfort him. Like I want to lay a hand on his arm, his chest, it's almost like it's second nature now to soothe him.

"No, it's okay," I think for a second, "I'll just call out to the servants to bring something, I don't have to leave the room, I can just open the door."

I don't why I know to reassure him, but I almost feel like I understand. I don't want to turn away from him either, and when I move back towards the door there's a churning in my gut like nausea as I walk away from him. I spin the combination and turn the knob, but I pause with the door halfway open to glance back at Ryu. He's standing where I left him, but I can see it's taking him an obvious effort to stay there. A muscle jumps in his jaw and his hands are fisted at his sides.

I refocus and poke my head out the door, spotting one of the caretakers in the hall.

"Excuse me," I call out, trying to get her attention, "Excuse me, can we have some food brought in?"

The caretaker gets up from her seat but she stares at me as I speak, her mouth popping open and eyes clouded in confusion. It takes me a minute to figure out why, and then I realize I'm speaking vanai and she can't understand a word.

"Oh...I mean, uh, we're hungry. Can we have some food and drinks brought in?" I say, this time so that the words are plain Songyin.

She relaxes and bows slightly, "Of course mistress."

She says politely and hurries to fulfill my request. I close the door and spin around, nearly yelping when Ryu's hand closes around my wrist and I'm yanked toward him. I crash into his chest and chains clink together as his arms close around me. Even though I'm surprised, something very soft blooms in my chest as I feel his nose in my hair and hear his heartbeat against my ear. I relax into his hold, oddly comforted myself by the embrace.

"Shit, this bond is going to be tough," He says into my hair.

I laugh and without really meaning to nestle closer, pressing my face to the bare skin of his chest, inhaling his scent. My sense of smell might not be as strong as his, but his scent still washes over me and makes that odd feeling of comfort settle deep inside.

"It is a bit strange," I admit.

"I'm not frightening you?" he asks, pulling back to look down into my face.

I shake my head, "Not at all," I press my lips together, "Is it odd that I kind of like it?"

He smirks, "That's the bond working on you too. You're not going to feel it as strongly as I do, but it will still mess you up if you're not careful."

"Hm, well if it's anything like- Oh!" I squeak as Ryu suddenly lifts me, scooping me up into his arms and carrying me back toward the center of the room with ease.

He grins down at me, dimples bracketing his mouth and eyes glinting, "Excuse me. I don't like you being so close to the door."

"Okay," I manage, not able to say much more over the large flock of butterflies taking off in my chest. Ryu sits, settling me in his lap, never once letting go or taking his arms off me. I find I'm quite comfortable, even though I can feel the hard evidence of his renewed arousal against my leg.

"I hope you don't mind," He says, though it doesn't look like he's going to be letting go if I do, "I would just feel a lot less crazy if I can keep holding you."

I can feel the small smile forming on my lips, but I don't move to push him away or try to get out of his hold.

"Does this go away eventually? All this mating bond intenseness?" I ask him.

Ryu thinks about it for a minute, "Actually, I think it just gets worse."

He makes a wry expression, but I don't comment.

I'm not sure why, but the idea of this continuing doesn't bother me. His touch doesn't bother me, and he doesn't scare me like maybe he should. I remember council lessons about how after mating we are supposed to leave immediately and only interact with the vanai when we're trying to conceive. You are supposed to be clinical about this, in and out. Don't antagonize, don't put yourself in danger. But I don't feel like I'm in danger. In fact, at the moment I feel quite content, and with Ryu's arms around me, I feel perfectly safe and protected. And I don't want to leave, not even a little bit. Ryu's the only vanai I've ever heard of having a conversation, and I want to know things.

"What is it like in the vanai city?" I ask him, "The council says vanai are solitary creatures and that you live nomadic lives, only interacting with each other to breed. Is that true?"

Ryu snorts, humor flickering in his eyes, "No. We are not solitary at all. We live with our families or with our mates, and we have friends and neighbors too, just like I imagine you do here."

I look up into his face, "You have a family back in the vanai city?"

He nods calmly, "I have a mother and father, grandparents, cousins. We all lived in one big house together, five families in total under one roof. One of my cousins was there with me at the hunt."

Something tumbles in my stomach, I catch my bottom lip between my teeth, "Do you have any siblings?"

"No," Ryu says, "More than one child is not common in many vanai households. Only the very wealthy can really afford to have more than one."

"There are class differences in vanai society?" I marvel, I'd never considered they were even capable of having societal differences.

Ryu's grin is knowing, "Yes. We have all the same conflicts and social norms as you do, in most things anyway."

My hands move idly, and I notice I've been mindlessly circling a mole on his arm with my fingertip. It's such a small and such a very normal thing, a natural deviation that makes him seem so mortal, and completely unlike the immortal, impossible being I was led to believe he would be.

"Will your family...won't they miss you?" I'm not sure why I ask, except that I can't stop thinking of it. I lift my gaze and see the small hint of longing in his eyes. It's brief, but it's like a punch to the gut and I want to shrink and vanish on the spot.

"Yes," He confirms, but his expression is soft and gentle.

"They won't come looking for you?"

He shakes his head, "They know better," He explains.

I don't know what to say to that. I feel like I'm chewing on sand. I'm saved from responding at all when I hear the combination spin and the door clicking. I look over my shoulder as the door swings open and the caretaker looks inside.

I jump violently as Ryu unexpectedly lets out an angry growl that rumbles through the room and vibrates against my chest. The caretaker shrieks and ducks back and I turn around with bewilderment to look up and find Ryu has his lips curled and his fangs bared, and his eyes are dark and fixed angrily on the door.

"Mistress?" The caretaker calls out from behind the door. Ryu snarls again at the sound of her voice, but this time I don't jump. I focus my attention on the door where the caretaker peeks around, her eyes wide and terrified. She sees me in Ryu's lap and I see the flash of terror in her gaze.

"Mistress!" she exclaims, "Should I call for help?"

This does not make Ryu happy, and his vicious growls increase in volume and aggression, his arms tightening around me possessively.

"No no! I'm alright! Everything's alright!" I try to assure her, having to shout over the volume of Ryu's growling. He's not directing it at me though, he's still staring quite threateningly at the invisible caretaker behind the door, but his arms are iron bars around me. Even if I wanted to get away, and I don't, I think I would probably have to paralyze him again to get free.

"Mistress, I think I should-"

"No, it's alright! I'm fine!" I shout again, worried she might run and get someone to tranquilize Ryu, which would definitely not put him in a good mood. The thought of anyone rushing in here to harm him has the hackles on my neck going up. I feel a snarl of my own rolling up my throat and I swallow it down, placing a hand on Ryu's chest to calm him. His heart beats frantically against my palm and his whole body vibrates with growls. It's making my stomach churn and something angry and very inhuman is working its way through my body. I can feel my fangs descend, licking the tips of them nervously.

"He's just being protective. I'm in no danger. Just leave the food inside the door!"

I can tell the caretaker hesitates, but fear wins out and a tray of food slides into the room.

"You can leave us!" I yell, because the action gets Ryu snarling with more force. She doesn't need more encouragement. The door shuts with a loud click, Ryu's growls start to simmer down but I want to get up and get us the food so I reach up and gently place a hand on his cheek. It seems rather foolish considering his fangs are still bared, but I don't feel a hint of fear and it works. Ryu's head jerks down to look at me. I didn't realize his eyes were glowing, but when his gaze falls on me he closes his mouth over his fangs and he blinks several times, dissipating the glow until his eyes are back to their natural soft brown.

He looks a little shell-shocked as he only seems to just realize what he was doing.

"Fuck," He curses and runs an agitated hand through his hair, "I didn't mean to do that."

"It's okay," I assure him, my lips twitching, "I know you didn't mean any harm."

He winces, "Do you think I traumatized that poor human woman?"

"I think she probably peed her pants," I giggle.

Ryu looks down at me with a lifted brow and a smirk, "You don't look the least bit sorry about it."

I shrug, "I guess I'm not."

I'm not frightened or alarmed by it either, I realize. It's not what I would call good behavior. I'm fairly certain that's the kind of display that will confirm many people's fears about vanai. I can't bring myself to care, maybe it's the mating bond, but Ryu's protectiveness is not a problem to me. If I'm being honest with myself, it was kind of hot.

A small burst of heat slickens the space between my thighs and I attempt to extract myself from Ryu's lap, turning away so he doesn't see the color on my cheeks. He snags my arm, snarling, and I whirl around to see the fangs and the glowing eyes are back.

"What was that?" He snarls.

I blink innocently, "What?"

He narrows his eyes, "I can smell your arousal, where did that come from?"

I don't even flinch from the harshness of his voice this time, instead, I feel the smile on my face as I lightly touch my fingertips to his lips, centimeters from the sharp tip of his fangs.

"Later. You need to eat, and drink. We have plenty of time for that later."

I'm not entirely sure I can reason with him in this state, his eyes are still illuminated bright like torchlight and his fangs are gleaming white, front and center, and he looks about ready to throw me to the floor and shove his way between my thighs. The thought of which makes my pulse jump and my skin flush, which does not help whatever he's scenting on me, most likely.

I look meaningfully down at his hand on my arm, "Let me go get the food," I say slowly, but I'm not asking.

I can see his jaw working, he's battling some inner impulse for several seconds, and he doesn't look happy about it, but he lets go of my arm. I hurry to grab the tray and bring it back, and Ryu's shoulders only relax when I sit down cross-legged across from him.

The glow fades from his eyes after a few minutes, but he doesn't stop staring at my face. I try to ignore it and push a bowl of rice and short ribs at him. We eat in silence, but he does oblige me by eating. I can't tell if he even feels hungry or if he's just on autopilot. I don't ask him, but I do wonder if vanai even feel hunger to begin with.

If they drink blood like the council says, what do they normally sustain themselves on? He had some of my blood earlier, so maybe he's not hungry? He doesn't seem bothered by the taste of mortal food though, scooping rice and clearing the plates happily enough without any hint of displeasure.

When I'm finished I return the bowls and utensils to the plate and I'm about to grab it to carry it back to the door when

Ryu kicks it out of reach. I gawk at him for a split second before I'm on my back, Ryu hovering above me. The words of protest die in my throat when he puts his nose to the crook of my neck, inhales, and then licks the juncture between my shoulder.

"Um," I mouth stupidly, losing my train of thought as his hands smooth up the inside of my thighs, moving beneath my skirt, pushing it up and out of the way. Ryu is placing light kisses along my collarbone, and my belly quivers as his fingers probe very familiarly at my core.

"I don't think you truly appreciate how much self-control it took to sit there and eat while I could smell you getting wet for me," He rumbles against my skin. My heart kicks up and I can feel myself let out a shaky breath as he feels along my slit with careful fingers, proving the presence of said wetness. I let out a little sigh as his long fingers push inside, testing.

Ryu groans and I want to whimper, to spur him into more.

"I need to taste you," He says hoarsely. I don't argue, I can't bring myself to do anything but press into his touch as he moves down my body. His hands push apart my thighs and he's on his knees as his face settles between them. His breath is hot and his tongue is making me shiver as he kisses the inside of my knee and moves inward. I look down my body, my throat working when I see the bright glow behind his irises. His fangs are out, and that should make me nervous considering their close proximity to some very sensitive parts.

I feel Ryu's breath on my opening though, and I'm looking straight into his eyes when he bends down and closes his mouth over my mound. I moan, unable to control it, the heat and wetness of his mouth throwing my brain into a fritz.

I feel like I'm already trembling with the need for release, but then I feel Ryu's tongue flick out and trail right over my opening, lapping up the wetness there. Then he reaches the apex of my thighs and his tongue finds my clit, and everything inside of me turns molten.

I cry out, arching into his mouth, my head thumps against the floor mats as he licks and sucks at my clit, sending sparks shooting through my bloodstream. I thread fingers through his hair, automatically pulling him closer. Ryu growls and the vibration of it against my clit is delicious.

I shriek, bucking up accidentally as I get lost in the small explosion of pleasure. Ryu's fingers tighten on my thighs, and he sucks harder on my clit, stopping only so that he can lap up the pleasure spilling freely from my cunt. It winds tighter and tighter in my gut, and my body feels flushed with heat and tingling all over with sensation. Then I feel them, I can feel the actual shape of his fangs brush against my folds, and maybe it's the danger of it, the thrill that it sends through my nerves. That and the last hard flick of his tongue, but I career over the edge.

I scream as sparks explode behind my eyelids, my whole body jolting bending beneath the force of my orgasm. My chest is heavy and I'm seeing stars as Ryu moves above me. I let out a small sound as he finally yanks my skirt free to make room. He positions himself at my hips, smoothly moving the chains attached to him out of the way so that we don't get tangled. I don't even realize he's moved his hands until he's tugging my shawl free too and then I'm totally bare beneath him and his glowing eyes are devouring the sight of my breasts, swollen and free for him to peruse.

His head ducks down and his mouth closes over a nipple. I throw my head back, holding on with one hand gripping the back of his neck as I lose myself in sensation. He shoves his other hand beneath me, lifting me slightly as his knees slide forward, and my mouth opens into an O as I feel the swollen head of his cock pushing at my folds, slicking himself up and then slowly separating me.

I do whimper then, and Ryu is making small, angry snarling sounds, his body bowed as he holds off so that he goes in inch by inch, allowing my body time. I need it, because the deeper he sinks the more pressure I feel, my body resisting his much larger size. But it's so good, and I'm a moaning mess, he's not helping as he goes back to sucking and nipping gently at my nipples, somehow expertly avoiding nicking me with his fangs.

When he finally slides in the last half inch we both groan as his hips go flush to mine. I move with him as he begins to rock, and then he's nipping at my neck and his hands are kneading at my ass. A switch gets flipped somewhere. I miss the exact moment it happens or which one of his actions does it. Maybe it's the way he avoids my mouth as he pistons forward, driving into me with his hips. Maybe it's partly that, but maybe I'm already halfway gone when he grips my hips and tries to flip me. I feel the change though, the moment instinct and blood takeover and the vanai female inside of me decides she's done with being submissive and pliant.

I feel the angry growl that rips free of my throat, but I don't have a way to stop it. It's like I lose control of my body completely as I spin, fangs bared, snarling up into Ryu's face as I come around. My hands grab at his shoulders, I'm not even sure what I'm doing, but all I know is I don't like being turned away from.

Ryu's fangs flash, he's deep in his feral state too, but both of us are beyond reason. He tries to regain control and I thrash. Suddenly I'm up, seated on his lap, my fingers have more strength than I've ever used before as I twist them in his hair, holding his head captive as I come up and cover his mouth with mine. He growls viciously, incensed by my retaliation, and my fingers scrape his scalp as he tries to pull himself free. Our fangs scrape against each other as we both snarl. He thrusts up, nearly unseating me with the force and his cock plunges inside of me. This pleases the strange alien force inside of me. I reward him by licking at his lips and rolling my hips down. He grips me hard, kisses me back and we fight for control with our mouths until I'm sure one of us is bleeding. It doesn't stop, it's like two boulders rolling downhill at top speed. The vanai parts of us have both taken over, and I understand what he meant when he said our earlier mating was mild. This one is wild and vicious, and we're both using bruising force and aggression as we fuck. With strength I didn't know I possess, I get Ryu under me, and I don't know where I get the idea but I cheat by grabbing the chain attached to his collar and holding him there as I grind my hips down onto his with everything I have.

Ryu's eyes roll up in his head and his chin tilts back as the pleasure rolls through him. I find I can't stop myself, I need more friction, and my hips are moving on their own, seeking it out.

"Fuck. Fuck I'm close," I hear Ryu through his growl. I get the wind knocked out of me when I wind up on my back again, this time with Ryu gripping both my hands and pinning them to the mats, using the weight and size of his body to hold me there as he pounds with merciless, bruising force into my pussy. I come alive with it, nipping at him, egging him on. Every cruel snap of his hips sends me higher and higher until it finally explodes out of me in whimpers and cries. Ryu roars as he comes, coming down so hard that his shoulders tremble.

Chapter Four

It is a while before Ryu lets go of my hands. He sits up slowly, and my mind is nothing but white noise and humming nerve endings as he pulls out and collapses back against the bench. I see him wipe at his mouth and when I look over I see him examining the blood on his hand.

"Yours or mine?" I laugh between pants, I'm still flat on my back on the floor looking up at him.

When Ryu meets my gaze his irises are back to brown.

"Could be both," He surmises flatly.

More laughter bubbles up my throat and a corner of Ryu's lips tick up, I can see the blood on them so it's highly likely it's his.

"Is that, was that...normal for your kind?" I ask him.

Ryu's brows lift, "Normally the battle for dominance is *before* the actual joining, but yes."

I flush slightly, "I didn't know I could do any of that. I've never...fought anyone like that before."

Ryu looks amused by this, "My fault probably. I got a little too excited and controlling. I probably triggered your fight instinct. Female vanai don't like to give up their dominance so easily. They want us to earn it."

For some reason, I understand exactly what he means. In the end, I didn't feel angry or upset when he pinned me, I just felt satisfied by making him work to get there. I've never felt the need to do that before, but it is oddly fulfilling. Like I've exposed a sexual nature I didn't know existed inside of me before.

I look him over, biting my lip, "I didn't hurt you, did I?"

Now Ryu is laughing, his eyes sparkling a bit as he shakes his head, "You should see what two truly dominant vanai can do when they're mating. I promise you it can be much worse than a little blood and some scratches."

"Hm," I roll my head so that I'm looking up at the ceiling, thinking. That was the most intense thing I've ever experienced. If I compared it to all of the sexual encounters I've had before, it was nothing like I've ever known intimacy to be. It should concern me, that I find that kind of violent struggle pleasing. Instead, it feels correct, like it fits.

After some time I sit up, roll my shoulders, and even though I was truthful in telling Ryu that I'm alright, I can feel the aftermath of our joining start to take effect. There are a lot of sore spots on my body right now that will likely be worse than sore tomorrow. It's late too, I look out the window and see it's dark outside.

"We should probably rest," I suggest, though I don't move to do anything about it.

Ryu stiffens and follows my gaze to the window. I see the troubled look in his eyes and the way he works his jaw and frowns.

"What is it?" I question, picking up on his hesitation.

He meets my eye, "You're going to leave?"

I blink a few times. It's the first time all night I've thought about my apartment upstairs.

"Well, I do have my own quarters upstairs. Don't you want me to leave?"

He shakes his head solemnly, "I don't think I'll be able to sleep. I understand if you want your space but I think I may be a little anxious if I can't see you."

Right, because of the bond. I purse my lips, I'm confused by all of this. I've never heard anyone talk about the bond this way, but at the same time. I don't want to leave him either. The more I think about it actually, the more the idea of falling asleep upstairs while he's down here by himself makes me want to hyperventilate. What is going on?

"I can just go up and change. Get cleaned up," I offer instead, "Then I can come back. It'll only take a few minutes."

Ryu doesn't look like he likes this idea either, but he nods agreeably. He still follows as I get to my feet and gather my clothing.

"You should get cleaned up too while I'm gone. It might make you feel better," I gesture at the attached bathroom. Ryu glances at it doubtfully and says nothing, his eyes looking increasingly more wary as I put my things back on and get closer to the door. He stays a few feet back, but I can see the tension radiating through his shoulders as I unlock the door.

"I'll be right back," I promise him, pausing with one foot in the hall. Ryu attempts a small smile, but it doesn't reach his eyes.

I close the door behind me and spin the lock, but something instantly knots up inside of me. I feel heavier and heavier the farther I get up the steps, and by the time I reach the apartment and shut the door on the hall my stomach is turning over and over.

Oh boy, I think, *I don't like this at all.* Anxiety climbs up my throat and I fight back the sensation as I get new clothes and make my way over to the shower. I try to relax and clean myself off, but as soon as I step into the spray thoughts start pounding against my skull.

He's alone down there. I think, *he's alone down there and anything can happen.* Of course, that's ridiculous, but there's pressure on my chest as I practically throw myself from the shower and towel off. Twenty minutes must pass from when I enter the apartment to when I start pulling on fresh clothing, and by the time I'm tying my skirt the distance from Ryu has become like a physical pain throbbing between my ribs. I feel like if I don't get back to him, if I can't see him and touch him this instant, then my head will explode. It's an actual tangible *need*.

The force of the desire scares me slightly. This bond is no joke, and it's making me breathe like a racehorse and my legs move faster as I practically hurtle back down the stairs. If I don't get back to Ryu this instant, I think I actually might become inconsolable.

I pause just as I get to the door, unsure as I hover over the doorknob. I want to just burst inside, but I remember how Ryu reacted earlier when the human caretaker came with our food. I don't think he would react that way to me, but I don't want to startle him either. There is a slot near the top of the door that opens over a small glass window, and I stand on my tiptoes and push it open to peer into the room.

I see Ryu immediately, he's showered, I can tell by his damp hair. Currently he's pacing the center of the room back and forth in agitated circles and raking a hand through his hair. He's worse off than me, and if I feel physically ill from being separated from him, I can only imagine what he must be going through. This pushes me to spin the combination and toss open the door, unable to take it any longer.

Ryu's head whips toward the door as I bolt inside and shut it behind me. He moves faster than I can blink and within seconds he has me crushed into his arms, my face in his hands as he kisses the last remaining breath from my lungs. I moan in relief as my insides realign themselves, clinging to his shackled wrist and nipping at his lips, almost like a reprimand for his absence even though it was ridiculously me who left the room.

Ryu is breathing hard when he pulls back to look in my face, but I can see some of the anxiousness already vanishing from the lines around his eyes.

"I'm sorry. I know I'm being irrational," He says, shaking his head, his wet bangs brushing against my brow, "I can't help it."

"I know," I tell him, and then I wrap my arms around his waist and bury my nose in his chest because the impulse to do so is too strong to ignore. Ryu shudders and wraps his arms tighter around me. I feel him place a kiss on the top of my head and then he's lifting me and carrying me back over to the bench where I'm guessing his chains have the most slack. He drops down without letting me go and then swoops back in to kiss me again, tongue swirling around the inside of my mouth once before he loosens up and lets out a breath.

"That was horrible," I say against the skin of his neck.

Ryu laughs quietly and smooths a hand down my back, "I agree. I thought I was going mad; I definitely would have gone completely feral if you'd been even a few minutes later."

"How do most mated pairs do this?" I muse, puzzled that something so strong could be so normal and that I'd have no knowledge of it. And according to Ryu it only gets stronger.

"Most newly mated pairs don't come out of confinement for months," Ryu chuckles.

"Oh," I mumble, but when I think about it, that doesn't sound like such a bad idea. I still haven't unwound my arms from Ryu's waist and there's a pressing need to just nuzzle my face against his skin and inhale.

Ryu exhales loudly and rubs at the bare skin at my waist, "I'd like nothing better than to rip those new clothes off of you and bury myself inside your sweet cunt, if for no other reason than to reassure myself that you're here."

My pussy spasms in response to his words and Ryu chokes off a half growl in response, "But," He continues forcefully, "If we don't slow down you are really going to hate me when your body catches up. We should sleep."

I nod silently, even though I too would like nothing better than to have him inside of me again. I shut my eyes and force air through my lungs, then I pry my arms away from him so that I can get up, Ryu looks ready to get up to trail me again so I hold a hand up to halt him.

"I'm just getting us bedding."

He relaxes, but I still feel his eyes on my back as I cross the room and throw the lid open on the chest next to the bare bed. There are blankets and pillows inside, and it strikes me as funny that these comforts are provided when no one but the vanai are supposed to sleep in this room. I don't even consider sleeping in the actual bed. It's there for the halflings to use because it's out of the range of Ryu's chains, and out of the question for me. There's no way I'm sleeping on that bed when Ryu is all the way on the floor.

I throw the blankets and pillows down and Ryu immediately works to spread them out and arrange the pillows. I lower myself onto the blankets and am pulling my hair over my shoulder, I feel Ryu's fingers on my back, and the next thing I know my shawl is being undone and tossed aside. I'm turning halfway around and Ryu already has my skirt untied and stripped. I gape at him and he grins cheekily back.

"I just want those out of the way," He says, and then he grabs me and pulls me down with him into the blankets, locking both arms around me and nestling me comfortably against him, my back to his chest, his thighs around mine. I laugh a little in surprise, and wiggle to get comfortable, but it only takes me seconds to relax, my body humming with satisfaction at his proximity and the safe feeling of being engulfed in his embrace. I'm asleep within seconds, his heart beating against my ear.

Chapter Five

I wake with a brain too foggy to remember where I am or what I'm doing here. I'm only semi-conscious when I recognize the hard shape pressed up against my lower back. My body reacts before I do, the adrenaline hits my blood and my thighs clench, my stomach hurdles and I'm moving on instinct alone as I flip over and straddle the waist of the male behind me.

I remember that I was sleeping beside Ryu at the same moment that he wakes, snarling, just as I get my hand around his cock. My fangs are bared inches from his face, and his eyes open with a glow. We go straight into battle mode, I'm not sure who's limbs are where for a few seconds as Ryu pushes up and tries to grab me and I push him back. I do feel victorious for half a second when I kiss him and he groans and bites at my lower lip, then he grips the back of my hair and catches me there as his hand winds between us and finds the slick heat between my thighs. I growl into his mouth and the fight is on again. It becomes a fierce wrestling match, chains clinking, teeth scraping skin, yanking and pulling and a grunt of pain as I get an elbow into his ribs, and then a defiant growl rumbles from his throat, and his hands are harsh on my arms as he flips me.

I end up on my hands and knees, my face pushed down into the floor mats, Ryu's body weight pinning me there as he kicks my legs apart with his knees, twists his fingers in my hair to hold me while I snarl, and then lines his hips up before thrusting in with one downward roll. I stop fighting, moaning into the floor as he pounds into me from behind. He keeps one hand on the flat of my belly to keep my hips high and at the right angle for him to push forward into. I can feel the whole length of his cock plunging me, driving into the sheath of my cunt and the wetness that collects there to help him. He lets go of my hair only to use the same hand to find my clit and rub into slow circles that start to increase in pressure and frequency as I plead and rock back into him.

"Shit," He rasps, which lets me know he's close, if the stuttering jerk of his hips didn't tell me. I beat him to the punch though with one pinch of his fingers and the blinding white light that takes over my vision as my body convulses around him. Ryu collapses over me as spurt after spurt of hot semen coats my inner walls.

We both slump over on the floor, gasping and heaving, sweat coats my skin and I can feel the heat on his. I feel it when he presses his brow to my shoulder and makes a low rumbling sound of abandon as he slides out of my pussy. He slumps down beside me, lying flat and turning his head so that I can see that even though his eyes are lust-hazed and overbright, they're a normal mortal brown.

He arches a black brow at me, and I can read the bemused accusation on his face. *That was all you this time*, it says.

"Oops," I giggle, giddy on the endorphins and afterglow of the coupling.

Ryu narrows his eyes at me, "That was very rude. Next time let a man wake up all the way before you go grabbing his stuff. Unless you like being pinned and ridden like a horse."

I grin back at him unabashedly, "It was an accident on my part too. Apparently waking up with a hard cock pressed against my ass is all the invitation my inner vanai needs."

Ryu grunts, sits up, and pushes the hair out of his eyes, "More vanai than I thought you would be."

I prop myself up on one arm and smirk, "Glad I'm able to surprise you for once."

Ryu turns to me, eyes glittering, "You constantly surprise me."

I'm about to reply that this entire experience has been unexpected to me, but Ryu goes abruptly rigid and his fangs flash and a low growl emanates through the room as his head whips toward the door. I straighten, and a second later a knock sounds.

"Mistress, I'll leave your breakfast just outside the door!" The female caretaker's muted voice comes through the door, close enough that I know she's purposefully speaking into the jam.

I place a stilling hand on Ryu's arm, he's still baring his teeth when he looks at me, but at least his eyes aren't glowing.

I flash him a wry smile and get up to go get the food. Ryu trails right behind me like we're connected by an invisible string, I find I don't mind it, not even looking back over my shoulder to check how close he is. I can just sense him shadowing me. When I kick the door closed and wheel around with the tray Ryu plucks it right out of my hands and carries it himself back over to the bench. His chains are long enough that he can walk up close enough to reach anyone who steps inside but can't touch the door himself.

I look down at the meal assortment as Ryu settles himself beside the tray. I wrinkle my brow but don't wonder out loud how the caretaker knew I was already in here with Ryu. She'd probably been watching all night. I know I'm not supposed to stay in here with him, but I don't worry much about it. The human caretakers might not like the vanai much, but they're fiercely dedicated to the halflings, and they're notoriously discreet. They'll never speak a word about what goes on in confinement. Doing otherwise would not only cost them their job but also might get them exiled by the council.

I sit and take the bowls of rice and chopsticks Ryu hands me, and soon as he sees I'm putting food into my bowl he focuses on feeding himself. I start to eat but then get distracted when I notice how enthusiastically Ryu's clearing his bowl. Unlike the night before, he's inhaling the food quite voraciously now, the hunger is unmistakable. I end up transfixed, I'm again questioning, what if anything, I know about vanai.

Ryu notices my attention and looks up, arching a brow.

"Something bothering you?" he prods, "You look a little confused."

I frown, I feel a little foolish for staring at him doing something so normal like eating, but the simple proof that he does, in fact, need human food gives me questions about the supposed knowledge I've been provided.

"It's only, nothing about you quite matches what I've been told about vanai," I admit.

His eyes get that crinkle of humor and he picks out another clump of rice with his chopsticks casually, "Oh yeah, like what?"

I tilt my head, "Well, for one, you eat human food."

His brows draw together like this is the oddest thing I've said.

"I mean, I didn't think you would need it. When vanai drink blood doesn't it sustain you enough not to need food? When do you need to drink blood then? And where do you get it if you live separately from humans? Don't you need to drink blood to survive?"

Ryu laughs, the sound coming out in a surprised burst, "Who told you that Vanai need human blood to survive?" he asks, a slightly bemused twist to his lips.

"Don't you?" I ask, wrinkling my forehead.

He sits forward, folding his hands together, a small smirk on his face like the whole conversation amuses him, "You are vanai, maybe less than half-blood, but still enough. Have you ever felt the need to drink blood? Ever been tempted to bite someone before?"

I narrow my eyes at him and his slightly condescending expression, "No," I say carefully.

"Don't you think if it was essential to our survival that you would at least be a little inclined toward tasting it?"

I stare at him, because even though what he's saying makes sense, it contradicts entirely with what I've been told about the Vanai as a species.

"We don't drink blood," He tells me, "At all. It's only the taste of it that has any effect on us, and only when it comes to our mates. We have fangs to claim our mates so that we can imprint on the taste of their blood. That's the only time we bite anyone."

I blink several times, baffled. I knew of course that the fangs were used in mating, but it had never occurred to me that mating might be the *only* thing they were used for.

"But, vanai do kill humans," I point out. This is undeniable. I've seen the bodies of the victims myself, with the clear evidence in the form of the unmistakable bite mark on their necks.

He winces at that, looking earnestly disturbed but also not denying this statement, "The human deaths are a result of depravity, not necessity. There are individuals out there who take a certain liking to mating humans. Only, nine times out of ten any intimate encounter between vanai and humans will end in the human's death, even the consensual kind," His gaze lifts to mine, "The original vanai that created the halflings were trying to prevent these kinds of encounters by creating a subspecies that could keep full-blooded vanai intent on misdeeds away from the humans. They were prepared and intentionally mated humans with precautions in place, the encounters were supervised by others to ensure the humans survived. Outside of these planned matings, vanai are usually too violent for human partners. We lose control, and even when the mating is mutual, the vanai still end up killing their human partners."

My mind immediately goes to our own mating, the good kind of soreness that covers my body, and ignoring the flash of heat that shoots through me, I can easily picture how a much weaker and much more mortal human would almost certainly not survive that kind of encounter.

"So....all those rogue vanai that go around killing multiple humans..."

"Are rogues to us as well," He confirms, jaw clenching, "And we can no more prevent them any more than you can prevent human rapists."

I have to take a deep breath and recenter myself, because while his words ring with truth, they put everything I've been taught into question. It puts my entire mission in life into question. He seems to guess the direction of my thoughts, his expression softening slightly with sympathy.

"It seems you were told many half-truths. My people are aware that the council warps both the human and halfling beliefs about us. Most of us avoid human settlements for this reason. We respect the purpose of the halflings, even if we don't volunteer in the making of them."

He's silent for a long moment, I can tell he's thinking about whether or not to speak, so I wait.

"Do you know the real reason that only halflings can kill vanai?"

My head jerks up to look at him, "Is there another reason besides immortality?"

He shakes his head, "Your immortality makes *you* harder to kill, but it doesn't give you some magic ability to kill *us*. The real reason is the same reason you were able to capture me. It is in your blood," He taps my wrist lightly.

"You carry the ability to disarm us. All vanai produce a pheromone that when scented by the opposite sex, renders them dormant. In short, we cannot harm our own females. And females cannot harm our males. It is the reason why your kind thinks female vanai are more aggressive. You have more female halflings than males, so when you do encounter a full-blooded female she would be immune to your effect, and therefore seems harder to kill."

I gape at him, "*Pheromones*? That's why you can't kill us?"

He nods, "It's a mating adaptation. It helps to make the males less aggressive during mating and more obedient to-wards the female dominants. But it also makes us entirely vulnerable to attacks by halflings, because your human blood prevents the same effect from working on you."

"Why..." I shake my head, "But why would the council hide that? Why wouldn't they just tell us the truth?"

He purses his lips, "The original vanai likely wanted to keep that fact secret so that it could not be used against them by the humans."

I feel unseated, thoughts and revelations swirling around my head. I get a flashback of the hunt and how confused I was when I attacked Ryu and he just stood there and let me. He was and is more than capable of defending himself, and yet all he did was absorb each of my strikes. He never attacked me. He didn't fight.

Something hollows out inside of me, because this truth unlocks a whole new host of realities about every encounter halflings have with the vanai. If it's true, then the vanai, at least not all of them are evil. They're just other beings, capable of the same emotions as us. Some good, some bad. It can't be true, it would paint our whole history, every vanai capture or kill in a totally different light. It can't be true, and yet...when my gaze searches Ryu's face I only see sincerity and empathy there. He's not lying to me. He has no reason to be.

I remember very distinctly the way he was during our first encounter. The slight tremble of his arms when he stood before me but didn't advance, like he wanted to fight but couldn't. I know, without really knowing how I know, that he is telling the truth.

That means that all of those vanai, the ones locked in the pens, the ones killed out in the wild on the hunts, not all of them were bad. Most, probably, were just living. And most, probably, couldn't fight back.

I put my face in my hands, shaking it back and forth, the weight on my shoulders suddenly tremendous. Ryu is there, scooping me into his lap and rubbing slow circles over my shoulders.

"Hey, it's alright," He says in a low voice.

"This is..." I lose the words to describe what I'm feeling, "All of those vanai, they were just killed for nothing. They couldn't even defend themselves."

"Listen." Ryu gently pries my hands away and lifts my chin with his fingers, "This isn't the fault of you or your peers, this is just what you've been taught."

"But it's all lies," I say, distressed.

"Partially." Ryu amends, "There is a reason the halflings exist, and my people know that. Remember I told you that sometimes we can go feral if we've been separated from our mates?"

I nod.

"When that happens sometimes the vanai seek out any way to relieve the feeling, and humans become an easy target. Sometimes vanai go feral when their mate dies and there's no way to fix it except to bite someone else. And sometimes in the worst cases, if vanai go too long without choosing a mate, they just slowly lose their minds. In those times halflings are the best form of protection for humans."

"But that's not always why we kill vanai," I argue, "The hunts. Those vanai aren't feral, are they?"

Ryu doesn't answer, but I can see the confirmation in the way he sets his jaw.

"What have we done?" I whisper, horrified.

Ryu's mouth forms a hard line and he brushes a thumb over my cheek, "It's for a greater good."

I gawk at him, "How can you say that?" I demand, "You're sitting here in *chains*. I had to drug you, you were mated against your will."

I start to feel a bit hysterical as it all settles in, the reality of what we've done. What *I've* done.

"Well, not completely against my will," Ryu smirks, and I can tell he's trying to comfort me.

I feel like crying.

"Don't you hate me? Hate us?"

Ryu blows out a hard breath through his nostrils and frowns, "No."

I look down at my hands, "How can you not?"

"Hey." Ryu says, stronger, "Look at me."

I do, but I can feel the tears swimming in my eyes.

"I'm alright," He assures me, "I'm not harmed, you've been kind to me, besides the whole attacking me and kidnapping me in the first place thing," He softens this with a wink and I choke on a sob.

He sighs, "To tell you the truth, it's not the worst thing that can happen to a man. Getting snatched up by a beautiful woman demanding you father her children."

I scoff and slap at his shoulder, "That's not funny!"

Ryu is laughing though, and his dimpled smile does help ease some of my mounting dismay. He wipes a tear off my cheek and kisses the tip of my nose, "Maybe I should be more concerned," He admits, "But I have to tell you, since the moment I saw you in the road, I was completely willing to be owned by you. I'm not upset by this mating at all."

I stare up at him, chest heavy but heart full, "But what happens when it comes time to leave confinement? They'll expect me to have you put in the pen."

The thought makes me want to throw up. I haven't given much thought to what happens after the mating just yet, but the idea of Ryu being locked away. Out of sight and out of mind, only to be let out when and if I decide I want more children. It disgusts me, it makes me want to take him and run. Far and away, as far as I can.

Ryu's mouth twists, his eyes go a little flat but he still holds me gently.

"Well," he hums, "We'll climb that mountain when we get to it."

He pushes a strand of hair behind my ear, "I knew where I would end up anyway, I always knew that might be my fate. But for now, we can enjoy each other freely, right?"

He sees the doubt and the deep dissatisfaction and decides to change the course of our conversation.

"I know this all comes as a bit of a shock to you." He says, and I let out a little gasp as he gets his arms around me and scoops me up, "But I can think of better things we can be doing than talking about things we can't change. We have all the time in the world again."

When he settles me down in his lap he quiets my protests by peppering my face and neck with kisses that make me giggle and squirm. I don't feel like I have the right to enjoy him now, not really, and my lungs contract with guilt when he looks down at me with soft brown eyes full of adoration I don't think I did anything to deserve.

I want to tell him so, but he doesn't give me the chance. He doesn't give me the space to push him away either, only pulling me closer and coaxing my doubts away by running his hands over my body and doing things with his mouth that make me lose track of anything but the way he makes me feel.

When he stops, what could be minutes or hours later, both of us are panting, flushed, and covered in sweat.

I feel better, or at least, too tired at the moment to focus too much on what's happening outside these walls. I know I'm going to have a more in-depth with Ryu about what all this means later, and I have questions for my people. I also have my thoughts about where my future is going and what might happen to Ryu if I have anything to say about it. It's too soon to decide anything though and no matter what I do I still have another month with Ryu in confinement before anything has to be figured out.

Chapter Six

I look down at both of our sweat-soaked bodies, Ryu is lying beside me brown eyes overbright and hooded with pleasure, cheeks pink with color. He looks vibrant like that, and not at all trapped or bitter like he should be.

Ryu's attention fixes on mine and he arches a brow, "Thinking again?"

I close my mouth and fidget with my hands. I don't want to bring it up again.

"I'm thinking," I say instead, "That we could both probably use a shower."

Ryu sits up and stares hard at the door, I can tell he's thinking about last night when I went up to my apartment. He won't say it but I know that he dreads the thought of me having to leave the room without him.

I look over my shoulder at the attached bathroom. There's no walls and no expectation of privacy, but that may be helpful while we're adjusting to the strength of this mating bond. If we ever adjust.

"I guess I could just shower here," I concede, liking the idea more than I'm willing to admit. I can see the immediate relief on Ryu's face.

"But you have to turn your back or something so I can use the bathroom. I need some privacy," I tell him, stern.

Ryu snorts and waves a hand at the bathroom, "Help yourself."

I get up and pick up a towel from the chest by the still-stripped bed on my way over. I see no indication that Ryu used anything the day before. There's a small sink and mirror that I lean over after relieving myself and I glance at Ryu in the mirror. He's honored my request of privacy at least, he's lying on the floor beside the padded bench, hands behind his head, staring up at the ceiling. He's so still he could be sleeping, except that I can see his eyes open and moving slightly across the lines of paint above his head.

I'm as quiet as I can be as I splash my face and hang up my towel before turning on the shower. I wait until I see steam rising off the floor and then step into the spray. Only a couple seconds in and I'm trying to run my fingers through my wet waist-length hair. A gasp of surprise gets stuck in my throat when a pair of hands appear from behind and smooth over my hips, I feel the hard length of the male body behind me as Ryu's face appears over my shoulders, his lips slightly brushing the bite mark on my back.

"That's enough privacy for now," He rumbles, voice vibrating as his fangs lightly scrape against my skin. I shiver and lean into him, tipping my head back onto his shoulder as his hands move down my thighs, one hand sliding in between, finding my wet slit and pressing lightly inside.

"I'll help you if you help me," He whispers and holds the other hand out in front of me. He's asking for the soap I realize, and I grab the bar off the shower shelf and place it in his palm. He withdraws his fingers from me and I wait while he lathers up the soap. I brace my hands against the tiled wall as he kneels and starts working the soap up my legs, I tip my chin down, meeting the intensity of his piercing eyes as he moves higher and kisses the top of my thighs before moving up. His hands are slow but gentle as they move up my body and when he reaches my breasts he stops to hold both in the cup of his hands, flicking his thumbs over the nipples and making my breath hitch at the teasing.

He pushes me back into the spray, using the same thoroughness to scrub my skin clean. When the suds are gone he blocks me against the wall, shoving a thigh between my legs and reaching down as he holds my eyes, feeling the sure, probing fingers. I close my eyes and let myself feel as his fingers circle and pinch at my clit, his movements and the warmth of the water are bringing me quickly to the edge, and when he bends down and takes the lobe of my ear between his teeth, again smoothly avoiding the fangs, I shudder and arch into him.

He kisses the space below my ear as he rubs a faster circle around my clit, then dips further and closes his mouth over a nipple. I come, water cascading down my front, bucking into his hand. When I open my eyes, it's the fixated look on Ryu's face and the glowing irises that make the small growl rise in my throat.

"Your turn," I pant.

I repeat his actions, and he helpfully leans back to give me space as I crouch down and work my way up. When I reach the apex of his thighs he's hard and ready for me. I glance up, find Ryu with his bottom lip caught between his teeth, looking like he's trying hard to hold still.

I grin wickedly and close my hand around his shaft, working it over with soap and tugging up and down the length. Ryu's head falls back against the tile and his black bangs become plastered to his brow in the spray. He doesn't notice anything but my hand working his length. I stop being gentle, when he starts to groan and roll his hips into my hand my vanai blood takes over. I'm on my feet and shoving Ryu's shoulder back into the wall with force, using my hand to pin him there.

Ryu lets out an "mmph" at the impact and curls his lips over his fangs in silent warning that my semi-feral consciousness ignores. I close my hand completely around the width of his penis and start to pump hard. Ryu snarls loudly in response, but it's past the point that he can reason or scare off my vanai instincts. I never finish soaping him up.

Another few seconds is all Ryu can stand, he's quicker this time, either too turned on or getting smarter at winning our battles for dominance. He grabs me, spins me, and slams me up against the wall, my face flat to the tile. He grabs a hold of my hair, which he's learned is apparently the most effective way of holding me in place, hoists one of my legs, lines and up, and viciously thrusts his hips up, impaling me on his cock in one sure movement. Our growling and groans of pleasure blend with the hush of the water, and the slamming of his hips brings me back to the edge. We go over together, Ryu shuddering as he pumps into me, his brow pressed to my shoulder, my body flush with the wall.

When we get out of the water Ryu whips the towel almost violently off the rack and wraps it tightly around my shoulders because I've started to shiver. He shakes his head to get the water out of his hair like a dog and I laugh through my chattering teeth. Ryu looks at me through his wet bangs and grins, then he picks me up like I weigh nothing and carries me to the bed where I squeak in protest and he ignores me as he covers me with the blankets.

"You spent too long in the water and you're not adjusted to this climate yet," He says, making a disapproving noise that I think is directed at himself.

"At least we're clean now," I smile, Ryu's still dripping wet and naked, and I'd wager even cold and shivering I'm much more comfortable than him being weighed down by all those chains.

Ryu quirks an eyebrow at me and then bends down so he can nip at my lips, "Next time we'll just lick each other clean," He growls.

I giggle and push him away, "Gross!"

"What do you mean gross?" Ryu wrinkles his nose, "I'd like to lick you all over again right now, just to taste you again."

I shriek as he dives beneath the blankets and goes for my legs, but my protests die soon enough when he finds what he's looking for.

Chapter Seven

It continues much the same through the afternoon and into the evening, interrupted only by the arrival of food several times and a nap break. It will be like this for a few weeks, but I know at some point I'm going to have to deal with the outside world. Many things don't add up and the more time I spend with Ryu, the more unsure I am about everything.

The world outside cools as sunset comes on, and I discover that the single window in the room, while it can't be climbed, can be opened from the inside to let in the fresh air. We push a bench over and Ryu and I sit beneath the sill at sundown and watch the sky change colors and the movement of the city in the distance outside. I've yet to come up with any good reason why I should leave Ryu's side. I don't want to, and I haven't yet felt that I have any reason to fear him. This mating bond thing is strange and new, and it's warping my mind and probably my feelings about what is happening.

There's a sinister part of my brain telling me that part of the reason Ryu is so serene about his captivity is that the bond is also affecting his mental state. Ryu, as perceptive as I'm learning he is, naturally notices the confliction on my face.

"What are you overthinking now?" he wonders, punctuating it with a crooked tilt of his lips knowingly.

I sigh and rub at my hands nervously, "I'm just confused about how this whole mating bond thing works. So many things don't make sense now that I'm experiencing it myself."

Ryu puts a hand under his chin, propping it up on a bent knee, "Such as?" He prods.

I look at him, "Such as my parents."

He lifts his brows, waits for me to elaborate.

I think about how to explain my family, "You know my father's human. Yet, vanai and halflings can't have children outside of matings. And then there's the mating bond itself. I didn't know that both partners need to be marked in order to complete it. I didn't know it was this all-encompassing thing or that it makes it impossible to be separated from your mate. That leaves me with a lot of questions already, but...my father, he can't mark my mother if he's human. How can they be mated?"

Ryu frowns, his eyes roaming my face while the thoughts churn visibly behind his, the time it takes him to answer makes me anxious.

"I wish I could answer those things, but I honestly don't know. We know the bare facts about halflings, but our interactions are limited to whenever we have conflicts, and obviously, any of my kind that are taken here don't come back," He has a dismayed expression and tips his head, "I've heard talk of it before. From our scholars who study human activity. From what I remember, it's a rough guess that halflings can't actually complete the mating bond with humans, but they can still produce offspring from incomplete matings, unlike pureblood vanai. I imagine, that human and halfling matings probably are not truly fulfilling for the halfling partner."

I tear my gaze away from him, feeling my brows draw together as I stare at the streaks painting the sky outside.

"You don't like that answer," He guesses.

I lightly shake my head distractedly, "It's not really that I don't like it. It's that it makes sense, and I wish it didn't."

I can feel him watching my face, but he gives me time to go on. I let out a breath and turn to him, "A few years ago, when I was a teenager, there was a big fight between my parents," I tap my fingers against one of the bars on the window while I remember details, "I don't remember much about their interactions when I was young. Maybe I chose not to remember or nothing significant happened for me to notice. But when this happened I was starting to become aware of where I fit into the world and the differences between my parents. Sharing partners is normal among the other halflings. Some of us have no interest in sexual contact with humans and there are only so many male halflings, so it's just inevitable that the males have to split their attention between multiple halfling females. Well, sometimes the sharing continues even after we've been mated. In the case of my parents, apparently, my father discovered my mother had gone back to one of the halfling males she'd had that kind of relationship with before she was mated," I cringe, "I guess she didn't find the mating with my father fulfilling."

Ryu's lips twist, "Did they split up?"

I nod, "It was pretty ugly. My father was heartbroken, he didn't really understand halfling culture and he couldn't understand why my mother couldn't love him the way he loved her. I couldn't understand it either, until now."

I meet Ryu's eyes, "This kind of bond is incomparable. I can't imagine how unhappy it would make someone to leave it incomplete for so long. But how did that even happen? I thought you said leaving the bond incomplete can drive someone mad."

Ryu hums and scratches at the back of his head uncomfortably, "If she were a pureblood vanai, yes. Eventually, the unfulfilled bond would make her go feral, in fact, I think that even a halfling could probably kill a human partner if they went feral. Except, I think halfbloods probably don't feel the effects as strongly. Maybe it's survivable to halfbloods, but I think that yes, eventually it can make one very unhappy, at the very least."

He looks regretful that he can't answer me definitively, and I feel a little guilty for burdening him with my lack of knowledge about my own kind.

"Sorry," I say, "I shouldn't put this on you. It's not your fault I don't know the truth about my own family, and it's not your responsibility to teach me."

Ryu laughs shortly and reaches out to smooth a hand over my cheek, "You're no bother to me. I just feel a little frustrated with your council for not giving you the information you need, and the truth. There might even be vanai out there who can tell you more useful information. I just wasn't a very good student," He smiles ruefully.

I chuckle and straighten to look at him fully, "What were you like in the real world? Outside of this confined space and not under the influence of either breeding drugs or the mating bond?" I'm curious, I see hints of Ryu's personality and little tidbits of what he must've been like in comparison to other vanai. But I know that who he is with me is not necessarily who he might've been when he was free, and I want to know. I never considered before that the vanai I mated might have their own story to tell, and now I want to know it.

Ryu thinks about how to answer that, "I'd like to think I've always been charming and likable, but I think my mother and elders would more likely call me insolent and impossible to teach," He grins.

I giggle and pull my knees up, getting comfortable, "Tell me about it," I request, "Your life before, tell me what the vanai are really like."

And I sit back and listen as Ryu offers me a look into his world, imagining the antics he depicts between himself and his school friends. About the seemingly normal pranks of teenage boys and the nature of young people that sounds not unlike my own. The more he speaks, the more I start to realize the vanai are not so different from us at all. In some cases, they even sound more like halfbloods than halfbloods seem like humans.

Chapter Eight

Two and then three days pass by in the same pattern, and it's almost a week since I first captured Ryu before anyone interrupts. By now, you'd expect we might be starting to feel the restraints of confinement, and while some things are inconvenient, mostly we pass the time rather quickly. Between our frequent couplings, we don't leave much time to do anything besides eat and sleep. When we do slow down, Ryu tells me stories about the vanai and his family and friends. I tell him what it was like growing up in Uthon and how it differs from Songyo.

In the evenings we sit by the window and watch the sunset and listen to the city move around us. You think I would be getting tired of it by now, but it's peaceful. I don't feel lonely and I don't find myself tiring of Ryu's company at all.

Quite the contrary, I feel even more unwilling to leave his side the more time I spend with him. The idea of sleeping anywhere but in his arms is repulsive, the idea of having my meals alone or without Ryu there to make me laugh and tease me is unappealing. I realize this is a problem, one I'm quickly going to have to consider the repercussions of, but I still have time, and I don't want to ruin our peace by spotlighting those looming issues.

I wish I could go out for a walk though, and I know that Ryu must be feeling a bit stir-crazy. Not to mention he's still in chains. Ryu doesn't complain, but every time he has to adjust to get the chains out of the way, rubs at the shackles on his wrists, or wakes up from the sound of the clinking chains I feel worse. I'd like to get them off of him, but I haven't discussed this situation with anyone yet, and I'm not willing to leave him long enough to address it. So we go on without acknowledging the situation.

It's one of those slow afternoons. And I sit in Ryu's lap, unwinding after our post-lunch coupling. Ryu lounges lazily back against the padded bench in the center of the room and I comb my fingers through the hair that usually falls into his eyes.

"Your hair's shorter than I'm used to," I state, running the silky strands through my fingertips to marvel at the texture.

A corner of Ryu's mouth curves, "Your hair's long," He retorts and tugs on a jet-black tendril.

I shrug, "The council doesn't let us cut it."

Ryu blinks several times, "They don't *let* you cut it?"

I snicker at his dumbfounded expression, "Something about 'maintaining an appearance', they want us to look more traditional. Like a..."

"Deity?" he finishes and twists his lips wryly, "The council likes to encourage humans to think of halflings as supernatural beings. I suppose if humans continue to think halfbloods are on the same level as gods then no one will question what the council does."

That's a troubling thought, and reawakens my new doubts about the council and just how halfling business is conducted. Why we're educated the way we are.

Before I have a chance to venture down that rocky road of conversation again, Ryu warns me of a disturbance by going still beneath me. I frown at him and then jump when someone knocks on the door, I look from Ryu to the door, but he's silent. No growling, his eyes are hard and wary though, his brow creased.

The door opens before I have a chance to grab my shawl and cover myself, I freeze, my bare backside toward her when Tama steps inside and also comes to a dead halt. Her feline eyes go slightly round as she sees me, my position, and Ryu beneath me. I realize instantly why she must be alarmed. Ryu and I are quite obviously just spooning, and I'm casually in his lap without any of the safety measures we've been taught to take.

I bite my lip, and Ryu's hands tighten on my waist. I can feel his pulse jumping beneath my palms and know he must be panicking slightly. Though I can't figure out why he's so still and quiet when he's usually rumbling like a tiger whenever someone so much as touches the door.

"Rin," Tama says carefully, like she's trying not to startle an elephant and eyeing Ryu with alarm, "What are you doing there?"

"Uh, isn't it obvious?" the sarcasm just slips out, a side effect of anxiety, but I regret it when I see Tama's shooting look and the way her eyes narrow.

"I think you should remove yourself from there, quickly," Tama advises, but it sounds more like an order.

Ryu's arms circle my waist and I let out a little breath of surprise when he pulls me tight against him. I look at his face, concerned. His fangs are bared, but he's still silently watching Tama instead of shooting up or going into intimidation mode like I'd expect by now.

This movement only serves to make Tama more flighty, I can see her quickly calculating how she can separate me from him and how to diffuse the situation before it becomes what she must think will be a lethal encounter.

I have to diffuse the situation before one or both of them decide they need to take preemptive action. I put a hand on Ryu's chest and push to give myself room, which makes his eyes shoot to my face and start to take on that glow, which will not help the growing tension.

"Shh," I hush him, placing a hand on his cheek and trying to coax the calm brown back into his eyes, dipping low so I can get him to focus on me.

"I should go speak to her. She doesn't understand what she's seeing, she's probably frightened."

Ryu doesn't like this idea though, and I can feel his whole body tighten beneath me, like a coiling spring.

"She's a friend, one of the halflings that came with me from Uthon. She's not a threat," I try again, looking for the flicker of logic and good humor in his slightly clouded gaze. I look over my shoulder, Tama is darting quick glances at the door like she's trying to figure out how quickly she could run out to get help.

The last thing I want is a big commotion and a rescue team running in here to upset Ryu even further. Not to mention it would make me quite upset as well.

"I'll just go speak to her and be back, alright?"

Ryu's eyes on me look more vanai than human at the moment, and I can tell from the radiating anxiety that the only thing that's getting through to him is that I'm about to leave the room.

"I'll be right outside," I promise him, "I won't move more than a few steps from the door, and there's a window slot on the door I can leave open so you can see me okay?"

When I get no response besides the dilating of his pupils and the quicker rising and falling of his chest. I grip him by the chin and press my brow to his, speaking directly so that he can't look anywhere else.

"Ryu," I say, firmer, "I'll be right back. Do you understand?"

I know that I'm basically trying to talk down a panic attack in an immortal being three times my strength and perhaps Tama has reason to think I'm in danger, but I also know Ryu's still in there somewhere, fighting down the instinct to go feral as much as he can.

I kiss him, nipping lightly with my fangs in the hopes maybe the small jolt of pain might get his attention. It works, he startles a little and I see the glow fading when he blinks rapidly, focus finally coming back as he stares back at me.

"I'll be right there, and I'll be back. Do you understand?" I repeat.

Ryu blows out a shuddery breath, but after a moment he closes his eyes to calm himself and nods.

"Let me go now," I say gently.

It takes another few seconds, and I keep my senses on any sound of movement from behind, but finally, Ryu's arms loosen and he allows me to peel myself away.

I stand and find my shawl and skirt nearby, pulling them on while Tama watches the entire exchange with sharply analytic eyes. I can feel Ryu shadowing me, but I don't acknowledge his following as I cross the room, keeping my back to him and my gaze on Tama.

Her attention is fixed over my shoulder at Ryu, expression quite clearly distrustful and her brow creasing further when I gesture her to the door and Ryu follows us the whole way until his chains stop him from going further. I stop at the door, feeling it like a punch to the gut when I see Ryu standing there, forlorn and eyes hollow, like I'm taking his whole world with me as I leave.

"It's okay," I mouth, and he nods again in understanding, but it doesn't ease his stricken look at all.

I close the door behind me, and true to my word I slide open the window at the top of the door. Tama is standing a few steps away and she watches me with an increasingly perplexed wariness.

"Sorry about that, he's just...protective," I tell her.

"Protective?" She repeats, gaping, "Rin, what on earth are you doing?"

I rub nervously at my arms and shrug, "Mating," I answer vaguely.

"You know what I mean," She snaps, "You're not supposed to be in there with him once the coupling is finished. That's incredibly dangerous. He could kill you, what were you think-ing?"

"He's not dangerous," I say, and she looks as though I've just said my hair is pink, "And he won't kill me. He can't."

Tama shakes her head, "Are you out of your mind?"

"Tama, it's not like that," I tell her, I run a hand through my hair, thinking where to begin, "Just listen to me, okay? We're not being told the truth."

Her frown is genuinely confused, "What are you talking about?"

"About the vanai," I make a hand motion back at the door, "They...the council are not telling us the whole truth. The vanai aren't what we think they are, at least most of them aren't."

"They're monsters Rin," Tama says flatly, her face clearly saying she thinks she's trying to reason with a crazy person, "Murderers. They kill people. They attack humans and suck them dry of blood and—"

"They don't drink blood," I interrupt.

Tama sputters, blinks, and then draws her brows together, "What?"

"They don't drink blood," I say again, "At all. The only reason they have fangs is to mark their mates. The only blood they ever even taste is their mate's."

Tama stares at me, "Did he not drink your blood? When he bit you? And I assume he's bitten you by now, probably more than once."

I shake my head, "He only bit me once. And I tasted his blood too. It was no different."

She opens and closes her mouth, "You...you what?"

"He eats the same things I do. He doesn't need blood to survive, I've seen the proof myself. The human killings aren't about survival at all."

"What are they about then?" Tama demands, "What reason did that monster give you for their slaughtering innocent humans?"

I give her a bland look, "There are bad vanai just like there are bad humans. Some of them try to mate humans, but vanai and humans aren't compatible. They're unfortunate incidences but not necessary. And Ryu's never killed anyone."

Tama's feline eyes become dagger sharp on my face, "Ryu? You know that thing's *name*?"

I sigh, I'm trying not to get angry at her because I know the way Tama thinks. It's what I thought not so long ago. I know she probably doesn't believe what I'm telling her and that it will be harder to convince her until she sees for herself. Still, I feel protective of Ryu, and it worsens the longer I'm separated from him. Even though I know he's just behind the door I can still feel the mounting anxiety, the pressure on my chest building, and the way I ache to have him behind me. To be able to see him and know he's safe by my side.

"I talk to him, Tama," I tell her, "Like I would with you, with Baku or Aksha. He's not some mindless, blood-thirsty animal incapable of reason. He's just another being like you and me. He's never tried to hurt me, he's never attacked me, not even when I attacked him first. We just have conversations, he makes me laugh and tells me stories. He's not a threat to me."

Tama looks incredulous, "You mean he hasn't hurt you *yet*."

I'm starting to feel exasperated, "I've been spending all day with him every day for a week now. I sleep beside him. If he wanted to hurt me he easily could have already."

Tama jerks back in surprise, "You...you sleep in there? With him?" She glances between me and the door, "Rin, how long have you been in there alone with him?"

I don't even bother to look repentant, I'm not ashamed at all of what I've done with Ryu, "I haven't left. Not since the first night."

Tama doesn't know what to say to this, and I can tell she's having an inner battle. She must realize on some level, that this shouldn't be possible, me being with him, talking to him, sleeping with him, if what we knew about vanai were true. She must realize something isn't right. It shouldn't even be possible to speak with him, and yet she's seen me do it, she's seen me turn my back on him without fear. All of this already contradicts what she should know to be true.

"Can you just trust me?" I ask quietly, "Have I ever given you a reason to doubt my judgment? I'm not in any danger. I know that for a fact."

Tama rubs the space between her brows, "How can you know that?"

I debate explaining everything Ryu did to me, but I think that getting her to believe it won't be easy if she can't see it for herself. It's something she has to experience.

"Because I've seen it. Believe me when I say I know him, and I trust my instincts."

Tama presses her lips into a thin line, "And what happens after?"

I look away then, because that's something I'm not yet ready to address, "I don't know. I just want to use the time I have to learn what I can. I'm just asking you not to freak out."

Tama sighs heavily and runs a hand over her face, "You're asking me to leave you in there, with that creature. Alone."

I lift my brows, "I can handle myself."

And Ryu is more than capable of taking care of me too, if he has to. I don't add.

Tama works her jaw back and forth uncomfortably, "You know I have to ask the advice of someone on the council. I at least have to tell them what is going on before they find out on their own."

They won't give her the truth, but I also know that there's not much they can do to interrupt a mating that's already started.

"I know," I relent, even though the very thought of anyone from the council getting close to Ryu makes me want to take up arms and stand guard outside the room myself.

Tama's not convinced, but I know she does trust me, and finally, she nods and seems to realize she can't convince me otherwise. She looks at me with slight apprehension, the skin around her eyes tight with tension.

"I hope you know what you're doing," She says, slumping.

"I do," I assure her.

Tama leaves me, and the moment she turns away I practically throw myself back through the door. Ryu is waiting predictably on the other side, and he catches me easily as I throw myself into his arms and lock mine around his neck, pressing my nose into his neck and breathing in his scent, calming my frayed nerves. His racing pulse tells me the feeling is mutual and he doesn't relax until we're resettling with me comfortably in his lap.

"What was that about?" he asks when the both of us have calmed the bond a bit with a few kisses and constant touch.

"Tama," I tell him, "She's a bit concerned."

"Because she thinks I'm a vicious blood-drinking demon?" he guesses, though his expression is mild. I'm glad to see his humor is back though.

I wince, "I'm not actually supposed to stay in here with you. It goes against the safety protocols we've been taught. It's supposed to be more of a 'fuck and get out of there' kind of thing."

Ryu throws his head back and laughs and I grin, I touch one of the dimples around his mouth and eye the tip of one of his fangs, now safely tucked away.

"You didn't growl at her," I note, "I've never seen you that calm when someone comes in."

He grunts and runs his tongue over the tip of a fang thoughtfully, "She was vanai. I couldn't do anything to her even if I wanted to."

That didn't occur to me, but it makes sense now, and it also reaffirms what he's already told me. I scoff and Ryu lifts a brow.

"What?" he prods.

"It's just," I shake my head, "I told her that you couldn't hurt me, but she didn't believe me. And yet she was seeing the proof for herself.

Ryu's lips twist, "I imagine it's probably not that easy to unlearn a lifetime of teaching. It's not her fault."

"So it will probably be the same for any female vanai right? You can't even growl at them?" I ask.

Ryu flicks a look over my face, "By default male vanai are instinctively submissive to females. We fight for dominance during matings, but for the most part, our females are the dominant ones. It's ingrained in me to be mild and un-antagonistic in the presence of females."

I sit up and stare at him, "Really?"

He smirks, "I know it's usually the opposite in the human world, but vanai females would never accept anything less than total control. They are naturally more aggressive and in our society families revolve around the matriarchal line. I, for instance, would have lived with my mother's family until I was mated, then I would have become a part of yours and not the other way around."

This is news to me, and not small. Though halflings run by different norms than humans, for the most part, our lives are still very male-centric. Most of the council is female of course, but only because there are simply more female halflings.

"Aren't male vanai stronger than the females?" I wonder, he certainly looks stronger. And he's bigger than our males. I've never seen a female vanai, but I imagine they'd still be slighter and lighter-boned than their males.

"Physically. That's why female vanai rarely leave our city. They believe that the manual labor tasks like hunting and building are male tasks. But it's the females in our world that form our leadership and govern the population," He gives me a meaningful look, "There are many different kinds of strength."

I can't argue with that. The anxiety of the interaction with Tama fades after a bit and Ryu and I get distracted with more pressing matters.

Chapter Nine

I know that it's coming, but when the next time someone comes knocking on our door I'm still filled with the same mix of dread and uncertainty.

I know from the way that Ryu goes deathly silent and still, sitting across from me now with his legs stretched out in front of him, watching me rearrange a board of pakdu checkers I had the caretakers bring three days earlier, I know our visitor is not human.

"Rin? May I come in?" the voice comes through the door. I recognize it as belonging to Yujin, one of the older halfling advisors. Not a council member, but one step below.

I glance at Ryu and make an apologetic face, "I better go talk to her," I say.

I don't want her coming into the room. Tama was one thing, but I'm not sure my inner vanai will be able to stomach anyone else seeing my mate as naked and vulnerable as he is now in those chains, unable to fight back or even cover himself.

I see a look of understanding in Ryu's eyes, though his jaw is tight with tension and he nods to let me know it's okay.

I get up, this time already wearing my shawl and skirt. Ryu doesn't follow now, which I think is probably an improvement. A testament that he trusts me enough to come back and that he's able to calm the instinctual need to be on my heels. It looks like it's taking everything in him to be still though, his fangs are out and his hands are fisted at his sides.

I vow to myself to make this quick as I duck out into the hall. Yujin steps back and looks me quickly up and down, clearly expecting to see signs of injury. There are in fact, finger-sized bruises all along the inside of my thighs and if examined close enough I'm sure there are more on the many spots I've been tossed, pinned, or generally man-handled (consensually). But they're nowhere she'd easily be able to see them.

Yujin is willowy and pretty with vanai bones and angled brown eyes, but she's not as transparent as Tama. I don't know what she's thinking as she examines me and probes my expression.

"I take it Tama has spoken to you," I start, folding my hands together in front of me. It was a wise choice on Tama's part, and tells me that she made an effort to keep my situation quiet. Yujin is the most easygoing of the advisors we've been exposed to, and the most likely to listen before getting the council involved. She'll evaluate the situation without making snap judgments, which is clearly why Tama went to her.

"Yes. She did summarize your current living situation and her concerns. You look well and unharmed to my eye, but can you explain to me what is happening?" She prompts calmly enough that I don't feel too anxious about telling her.

"Nothing, we're just mating," I shrug.

Yujin tips her head to one side, neatly combed black hair sliding over the shoulder of her silk blouse, "You're aware that you are not to remain in the room with the vanai once you've finished coupling?"

I nod, "I know. But I would prefer to stay. It makes me anxious to be away from him for long," I admit, thinking this should be self-explanatory.

Yujin's eyes immediately narrow, "What do you mean it makes you anxious?"

I shuffle slightly, "It's uncomfortable. It's worse for him obviously, but the bond makes me feel a little edgy if I can't see him or I'm away for too long."

Yujin blinks several times, "The bond?"

I frown at her, "The mating bond. After we completed it, the bond made it nearly impossible to do–"

"Wait," Yujin holds up a hand and stares at me, "You mean to tell me you completed the bond? How?"

I start to feel a little as though I'm speaking in circles but I explain slowly, "After he marked me, I marked him."

Yujin's jaw drops, "You mean to tell me you *bit him back*?"

My brows draw together, "Was I not supposed to?"

"No, of course not," She gapes.

My mind whirls, this whole time I'd just assumed that no one had spoken of the bond before because it was a given. Now it's starting to dawn on me that this is not the norm at all.

"Then the other halflings...they don't complete the bond? Ever?" I'm sure I must look stunned.

Yujin looks equally as cautious as she says, "Once you complete the bond it's permanent. You will not be able to leave the vanai for more than a few hours at a time and you can not have any other partners again," She examines me, "How did you manage to do it?"

I feel like I'm understanding less the more she talks and shake my head, "What?"

"Bite him."

I furrow my brow, "He asked me to."

She reels back, and I feel like I'm existing in some totally different reality than everyone else. Clearly, this is not coming off as factual as I think it is.

"You speak to him? The vanai?"

I put a hand to my head, "Um, yes?"

Yujin's looking as thunderstruck as I feel, "Rin, you realize this is unusual don't you?"

"I'm starting to get that impression, yes," I reply mildly.

Yujin turns around, starts to pace a little.

"So, what happens now?" I question, chewing on my lip.

Yujin stops, blows out a breath, "I'm not sure. You will have to be allowed to be able to have access to him once he's in the pen of course. I just can't remember ever hearing of the procedures to be taken when one of ours marks a vanai."

"The council has no grounds to tell me how I should be handling him," I point out.

I've thought this possibility through already. I know enough about halfblood laws to know that once I've marked him, Ryu is considered mine. Halflings are vanai enough that trying to get between mates is considered an unthinkable crime. They've taught us how we should behave during mating, but they can't enforce procedures if we refuse to follow them. Or maybe they could, until I bit him and claimed him as mine.

Their written laws weigh nothing in the face of thousands of years of vanai instinct bred into my blood.

"No," Yujin agrees, "Now that I know you've completed the bond, it would be uselessly stressful to try and enforce safety measures if you won't agree to follow them."

Yujin looks troubled as she addresses me, "You must also keep in mind that if something happens to you, we may not be able to help you in time. We cannot monitor your interactions constantly. If you choose to stay in the same space as the vanai and he turns on you, I'm afraid it may be too late before any of us would be able to come here to intervene."

I grin wryly at that, "I have nothing to fear from him," I tell her confidently.

Yujin looks entirely unconvinced, but she doesn't argue with me. My shoulders feel heavier when she leaves, Ryu is waiting where I left him, but he reaches out and pulls me into him when I return. When he sees the look on my face he straightens and frowns down at me.

"What's wrong?"

I lift my chin, something twisting in my chest, "The other halflings don't mark the vanai. They don't complete the bond."

Ryu's forehead creases, thoughts flashing behind his eyes.

I swallow thickly and voice the thought that's been weighing me down most, "The vanai still feel the bond though, don't they?"

Ryu nods, his face stricken. I think of how terrible it feels to be separated from Ryu, of the way he nearly goes crazy any time someone comes near me. I remember him telling me the breeding drug is a sped-up effect of what an uncompleted mating bond would look like. And how that would eventually drive someone out of their mind. How much pain they would be in.

I meet Ryu's eyes, "What happens when a vanai goes feral and can't find relief?"

"They would slowly lose their minds," He says simply.

I inhale slowly, "What are the chances that all those vanai locked in the pen would survive that?"

He gives me a pained yet quietly empathetic look, "Not high."

Gods. I shiver and drop my head against his shoulder, "Ryu," I breathe out.

He places a hand on my back and smooths it down my spine, "I know," He quietly coaxes me.

The crimes between our two interconnected species are mounting, and I know there's nothing I can do. I have information I almost wish I didn't. I also have a looming burden over my own future. I can't imagine going through with what I'm supposed to do. I can't imagine doing that to Ryu, or myself. I don't know what to do, I don't have the right answers. Neither does Ryu, and he doesn't try to make suggestions. He just holds me while we both silently grieve about all the vanai, the ones not unlike him who never harmed anyone, and the hell they must have gone through in the pen. Locked away from their mates, their families, and their people, living a half-life until they finally faded away.

Chapter Ten

I have no way of knowing if Yujin spoke to the council, or if anyone else is aware of the peculiar relationship between Ryu and me. In any case, Yujin's words turn out to be true. No one else comes to intrude on our quiet safe place together. The human caretakers come and go each day with barely audible knocks and trays of food that appear and reappear throughout the day.

Occasionally I summon them to retrieve things from my apartment or bring us various forms of entertainment so I don't have to leave myself. The confinement room is starting to look less like a cell and more like a shared living space. Various board games and books now crowd the corners. There are blankets and pillows on the floor, towels in the bathroom along with more personal hygiene products.

Two weeks have gone by before I really start thinking about what is going to happen after. I don't voice my thoughts to Ryu only because I don't want to make him distressed if he has no reason to be. I don't know if he has reason to be. I'm sure he's thought about it himself, and maybe like he said, resigned himself to whatever happens right from the start. I don't know if I can resign myself to it though, no matter how difficult or maybe even impossible the alternatives may be.

"I want a redo." I declare, facing Ryu down across the floor. We've been talking about the day I first brought him in, and how I suspected that Ryu might be a stunning fighter when he's truly using his skills. He says he is of course, but talk is cheap.

Ryu snorts, he's sitting on the floor with one knee propped, an arm lazily slung across. I have a very tasteful view of his package from this angle, one that I'm sure he's aware of and is seemingly completed unbothered by.

"I can't fight you," He states, not at all inclined to get up and acknowledge my poised and excitable fighting stance.

"Sure you can," I insist, "We have no weapons, and your intention isn't to harm me. It's like when we fight for dominance. If your intent is only to overpower and not injure, I think we can try it out."

Ryu looks bemused, but finally, he shrugs and gets to his feet, "Do you really think it can be fair this way?" he asks, holding up one of his still shackled wrists in illustration.

I bite my lip, thinking. The chains seem laughably unnecessary to me now. I know Ryu's not going to hurt me, and even without the chains, he can't open the door. Not that he'd go anywhere, at least not without me. The worst he could do is throw me over his shoulder and run off into the wilderness with me. And would that be so terrible?

I don't have the council's clearance to free him. But then, I didn't have the council's permission to stay in this room with him either. I don't think Ryu believed I would actually do it. He looks a little wide-eyed when I go to retrieve the key from the control panel and return, lifting his arm so that I can fit the key into the lock on his wrist. I unlock one arm and then the other, the metal cuffs falling to the floor with a thud and a clink of metal links. I unlock the ones around his ankles next. I detach the chain attached to the collar around his next but I don't have a key for the collar itself. The collar serves more as an identifier than a restraint. It's kept on in case one of the vanai escape so that they can be identified from the halflings. The key to the collar is somewhere in the council building.

I step back and watch as Ryu rubs at his now bare wrists, gazing at me with a somewhat drawn look. I cringe as I see the ring of raw skin the cuffs have left behind, clenching my teeth so I don't cuss. I should have taken them off earlier, I think. It looks like those marks might leave scars, and I already know they're going to incense me every time I see them on his otherwise unmarred skin. The one on his right wrist is only inches from the two small round scars left behind by my fangs, and that makes me even angrier.

Ryu must sense my growing anger because he drops his arms and motions me forward, "What's the incentive for winning this little wrestling match?" he asks.

I arch a brow at him, "Is the glory of defeating me in battle and retribution not enough incentive?"

Ryu grins broadly and shakes his head, "Much more fun to let you win just so I can see your cute little face when you win."

I scowl at him, I want a fair fight.

"Fine," I sniff and think about it for a moment, "Then let's make it a fair odds too. Loser picks the prize."

Ryu pouts, "That doesn't sound fair at all."

I smirk at him, "Oh trust me, I think you'll want the prize I have in mind."

Ryu's brows shoot up and a thoughtful look of consideration passes over his features.

"Take it or leave it," I say impatiently.

Ryu sighs heavily, "Alright, alight," He lifts a finger as I get into position opposite him, "But no kicking, *or* biting."

I roll my eyes but jerk my chin in a nod, "Ready?"

We count to three, and when he moves I'm happy for half a second that he's taking this seriously, and then I regret it when he almost immediately takes my legs out. I cough and jump back to my feet, but I can't keep track of him. Despite being chained and essentially immobile for three weeks, Ryu is all speed and predatory grace. I can't get a hand on him and he dodges me instantly and then doubles back by nearly knocking me off my feet again. I leap away from him but his reach is longer and it does devolve into basically a wrestling match. The snarling starts up without my realizing it, I remember agreeing not to bite him just as my fangs descend. Ryu's are out too, but he's smiling with him, apparently having fun and not at all as frustrated as I am that I can't even get a hit on him.

We exchange blows, but mine don't even glance off of him, he's only toying me. Easily holding me back and dodging out of my way. It makes me furious and has me spitting and snarling. It only lasts a minute longer, and then Ryu grabs me and tosses me down onto the mats, coming down hard on top of me and catching both of my hands in one of his. I feel his breath against the back of my neck, I growl into the floor and wriggle beneath him, but his thighs are iron solid and tight on the outside of mine and I can feel the hard shape of his arousal pressing into my back where he holds me down. He has me, easily. He's not even using all of his power to hold me there, I realize, his breathing sounds free compared to mine. It's jarring to feel the evidence that he's probably three times stronger than me. And not a little bit arousing.

"Got you, little mate," He growls in my ear.

I grumble something unkind and he laughs easily as he lets me go. Backing up so I can push up and brush myself off, glaring. He has a wide beaming smile on his face, dimples, fangs, and all.

"So," He purrs, "What do I win?"

This brings a wicked grin to my face and a suspicious glint into his eyes.

I crook a finger at him and gesture to the padded bench, "You'd better sit down."

He looks understandably apprehensive, to which I wait patiently and nod in encouragement.

Ryu sniffs but humors me by turning and lowering, his back hitting the back of the bench. I make my way over to him, knowing the intent must be shining in my eyes by the increasingly cautious look in his. I kneel in front of him, immensely enjoying the fascination on his face and the way his body responds to my touch as I push his legs apart.

"What are you—"

"Shh," I interrupt as I crawl forward and settle myself between his thighs. I know it's supposed to be his prize, but I feel like I'm the one winning as his lips part and I see the way his eyes shutter as my hand closes around the base of his shaft. I hold his eye and I'm rewarded when I see the flash of his fangs and the glow behind his irises as I bend down and close my mouth around the head of his cock.

He growls and curses viciously as I take him into my mouth, lapping at the underside of his length with my tongue. I laugh around him, making more vibrations that make him gasp, and I relish the sight of his stomach muscles clenching, his body bowing as I take him all the way to the back of my throat. He's too big for me to get all of him inside of my mouth, but I make up for it by fisting both my hands around him and working in tandem with my bobbing head and expertly swirling tongue.

Ryu groans and his head falls back in ecstasy, his fingers tangling in my hair. My belly tightens at the sight of him arching into the ministrations. The tip of one of his fangs dents his bottom lip, and I can see the veins stand out in his throat as he tries to keep his grip on control. I can feel the tremble of his muscles under my hands as he tries to resist the urge to thrust and choke me. It's a delicious sight, and I could drink in this image thirstily, Ryu lost in pleasure and struggling for restraint, even his fingers flexing and unflexing at his side. This is the first time I've ever taken him into my mouth, he was always more insistent about tasting me before.

Now I curse myself for not doing it sooner, because he's absolutely heart-shattering like this. Tragically beautiful with his eyes shuttered and his breath coming out in bursts. He doesn't last long, I think he surprises himself when I suck him down hard and he comes, shouting, fangs bared. The force of his release nearly chokes me, but I swallow down every drop and then wipe up the spilled excess from my lips, only to lick it off my fingers.

Ryu watches me with hungry, vividly glowing eyes, chest heaving, and hair wild. He watches me clean my fingers of his seed, savoring. I squeak with protest when he suddenly barrels me over, pinning me to the floor and going at my lips with vigor as his hands tear at my clothing. It doesn't matter that he came only minutes ago, within moments he's buried deep inside of me, pounding with abandon until the both of us are breathless and buzzing with endorphins and release.

Chapter Eleven

The chains stay off, and a few days later when I ask the human caretaker for male clothing, she gapes at me as if I've just asked her to set the place on fire. She comes back with my request though and I watch as Ryu pulls on the trousers and navy-blue robes. The color suits him, and as much as I'll always enjoy the sight of him bare and gloriously naked, I also like the sight of him in the Songyin silk, dressed and handsome.

He looks over at me uncertainly as he ties the sash around the robes, "Are you sure this is a good idea?" he asks again.

I find it marginally comical that he's the one questioning my desire to finally get him out of this room and get us both some much-needed freedom.

I'm not sure about anything at this point. This can go one of several ways. The neck of the robes partially cover up Ryu's collar, but it's still visible to anyone who looks close enough, and that can be a problem if people identify him as vanai. I don't think it's anything I can't handle, but it does make me nervous too. I haven't cleared this with the council, which could also be a problem. At this point though, I'm not sure asking their permission is either necessary or useful. I just know I want to try. Maybe it will help me make some difficult decisions.

I shrug, "You're not chained up anymore, and I see no point in keeping you locked up in here. You're going to be with me anyway, you're not a threat to anyone unless they're a threat to me."

Ryu darts a look at the window, "Yea, do *they* know that though?" he asks doubtfully.

I shake my head. Ryu doesn't question it further, and I take a deep breath as he joins me at the door and I spin the combination. Several of the human caretakers are watching when we emerge together from the room for the first time in weeks, but they don't move to stop us. One of them might go inform the council I've taken a vanai out into the general population for an afternoon walk, but I know they won't talk otherwise. As long as no one recognizes Ryu for what he is, we should be relatively safe.

I can feel Ryu's nervous energy, and he stays at my shoulder as we leave the confinement building and melt into the traffic passing by on the street. The bond comes in handy in this way, because I can always sense him a few inches away and know he's there without having to constantly look for him.

He swivels his head back and forth nervously as we make our way toward the city center where the crowds are thickest. Anxiety claws at my insides, but the humans we pass are busy with their lives and they don't pay us much attention. No one has noticed Ryu yet. It helps that I'm also a stranger in this city and so most of the humans are as unfamiliar with me as him and probably just assume he's another of the halflings from Uthon. We walk for about thirty minutes without incident, and Ryu is finally starting to relax as we reach the market.

I look back occasionally to give him encouraging smiles, and the bustling energy of the market soon distracts us. We look around, Ryu leaning over my shoulder to talk when we come upon something interesting. We get some street food and talk as we walk and eat. He's starting to laugh and look more at ease. I haven't seen any other halflings yet, and I make the mistake of thinking maybe we'll be able to get through the afternoon without a confrontation.

I'm inside the booth of a seamstress searching for more robes for Ryu, he's waiting on the street a few steps away, calmly watching me browse. I see them first, Aksha and Baku emerge from the crowd outside, and I tense up. It looks like they might just pass by at first, but then Baku notices Ryu, and of course, he recognizes him.

Baku elbows Aksha and nods at Ryu, and the two beeline for him.

"Damn it," I mutter and try to hurriedly pay the seamstress, who is packaging up the new sets of robes I picked out. Ryu hears me and notices my alarm and turns around just as Aksha and Baku approach him. He recognizes them too, though the only sign of it is the slight stiffening of his shoulders. Otherwise, he watches them approach with little to no reaction, his arms folded over his chest, leaning against one of the roof beams.

"Who let you out of your cage, bloodsucker?" Baku snarls, making no bones about getting right up in Ryu's face. Ryu, to his credit, merely arches a dark brow. Apparently, he does not see male halflings as threats. Can't say I blame him, Baku is nearly a head and a half shorter, and Ryu is much larger in muscle mass.

"You shouldn't be wandering without chains," Aksha adds, looking just as disconcerted by Ryu's seemingly unbothered and untethered appearance.

"I'm not about to take a bite out of anyone that doesn't provoke me first," Ryu tells them calmly, "You can save your concern."

"Oh, we're not worried about that." Baku laughs, "We're more than capable of taking care of any rogue pureblood."

Aksha narrows his eyes at Ryu, "How long have you been wandering the market unrestrained?"

"He's been out all afternoon doing nothing but helping me pick out silk colors and finishing my snacks for me," I say loudly as I make my way over, the new robes packaged and tucked safely under my arm. Aksha and Baku turn their attention to me, Baku gives me a disapproving once-over that makes my hair stand on end.

"And who gave you permission to let him loose?" He demands.

Ryu has begun to look a little less pleasant now that the two males are focused on me.

"I don't need anyone's permission," I snap, "He's my mate, and I'm more than capable of taking him on a simple walk with me."

"You're putting the lives of every human in this market in danger," Baku seethes at me.

"The only one whose life is in danger is yours if you don't stop snarling at my mate," Ryu interrupts, stepping between us because Baku's eyes are starting to flicker and I can feel my own temper curdling.

Baku sizes up Ryu and opens his mouth over his fangs, "Is that right, leach? Maybe Aksha and I should send you back to confinement in bandages and teach you a lesson on speaking out of turn."

A growl climbs up my throat, but Ryu is smirking.

"You'd have to put me in chains first for the two of you to even stand a chance."

Baku snarls and wields his fangs uncomfortably close to Ryu's throat in a very clear threat. Instead of flinching Ryu simply curls his lips back, and it's almost laughable. Even fully descended, Baku's fangs are only a quarter of the size of Ryu's. Not that the knucklehead lets that deter him from continuing to growl at him. Ryu actually laughs in his face.

"Put your baby fangs away, little halfblood," He chuckles, "They're not going to win you any battles, and especially not with me."

This, naturally, incenses Baku, and he lunges for Ryu.

I don't make the conscious decision to move, but I do feel my fingers closing around Baku's throat at the same time his back hits the wall of the booth where I've slammed him into it, and I hear the vicious growl that comes out of my throat as my fangs nearly pierce his neck. I hear Aksha's shout of protest and Ryu's answering snarl as he holds him back. I don't look back at them, my gaze is on Baku's stunned face as the animalistic rumble comes with my words.

"Touch my mate again and I will filet you."

Baku gapes at me, and I see from the reflection in his eyes that mine are glowing. Oops.

"What is going on here?" The voice breaks me out of my angry haze as Tama parts through the crowd that's gathered to watch the confrontation. She stops, looks between Ryu calmly holding back a flustered Aksha, and me holding her brother by the throat and pinning him to a wall. Tama's brows go up but she surprises me by addressing Baku first.

"What have you done now?" She asks, exasperated.

I let go of him, and Baku gawks at his twin, offended, "Me? She's brought her vanai pet out into the marketplace!" he exclaims, flinging a hand at me. I keep my fangs bared and issue another warning growl.

Tama flicks a look at me and then returns her impatient gaze to her brother, "Do not start fights with vanai in the presence of humans," She says in a lowered hiss, "And never go after someone's bonded mate unless you want to die you *fool*."

"Bonded–" Baku mouths and then his eyes fly to Ryu, searching his appearance. I see his eyes land on Ryu's exposed wrist beneath his sleeve, at the scars left behind by my bite.

His gaze swings back in my direction, wide and incredulous, "You didn't."

I glare at him, "It's none of your business," I say between clenched teeth.

Baku looks around wildly, imploring his sister while pointing accusingly at me, "She's out of her mind!"

Tama must've had a conversation with Yujin, the fact that I've marked Ryu doesn't seem to be news to her. She rubs her head and says measurably, "This isn't the place to discuss it," She turns her head to look at the gathering crowd of humans.

Noticing them myself, I take a step closer to Ryu. They're all eyeing him now with noticeable displeasure. They've definitely identified he's vanai now, and the source of our conflict.

"Rin," Tama says, "Take the vanai back to your quarters."

I don't argue with that, gripping Ryu by the wrist and pulling him away from a shell-shocked-looking Aksha.

Baku looks at me like I've betrayed them, "How could you?" he says, shaking his head.

I snarl and Tama gets between us, shoving her brother back forcibly with two hands on his chest, "Enough," She snaps, giving Baku a hard glare, "We'll address it in private. Take it away from the humans Baku."

He looks like he's chewing on sand, but he turns and lets Tama herd him in the opposite direction.

Chapter Twelve

I take Tama's advice, but I don't take Ryu back to confinement. Knowing Baku, he's not going to be mollified by his sister's words. I've wounded his pride, in more than one way. I take Ryu instead back to the house in the halfling quarter that is mine. It's the first time I've been back in weeks, and when we step inside Ryu looks around for a minute, but the space isn't large, for all that it is quite nice and larger than most human houses in the city.

His focus isn't on my home though, he's correctly interpreted the undercurrent beneath the confrontation with Baku and he brings it right up, not one to mince words.

"You've lain with that halfblood male haven't you?" He asks calmly, "The one with the cat eyes."

I almost laugh at that description, but I don't bother denying it. When he sees me nod Ryu's expression darkens, and I can see him working his jaw.

"What?" I say defensively, "I doubt you were celibate before we mated either."

One of Ryu's brows tick up, but he doesn't take the bait on that one, "It's not that," He assures me, "But that male is going to take it personally."

"And?" I press.

"He'll be trouble." He warns.

It's almost prophetic. Ryu's still watching my reaction when someone pounds on the door. He scowls at it, but I was expecting it sooner or later. Though I was hoping by coming here instead of confinement we might have a few moments of reprieve. Guess not.

I sigh and move to open the door. Baku blows into the room, wheeling around as Tama follows on his heels, her annoyance at having to be here as the mediator clear on her face. Baku looks at me and then at Ryu, watching placidly from a corner of the room. For whatever reason, he does not view Baku as a threat at all now. He barely looks as though he's interested.

"You've brought him into your home?" Baku questions, gaping at me and wearing a disgusted expression on his face that immediately has my hackles rising.

"I don't see a reason not to," I mutter mildly, "Considering we've been living in the same space anyway for the last three weeks."

The cat eyes that Baku shares with his twin narrow on me, "Living? You have been *living* with a vanai?" his gaze seeks out his sister, "Did you know about this?"

Tama lifts a brow and wrinkles her nose, "She swears he's not a danger to her."

"And you believed her?" Baku scoffs.

Tama shrugs, "Seeing as how she's unharmed and he's been free with her with no incident I'm starting to think she might be right. He didn't even maul your stupid ass for getting in his face, not that I'd have blamed him," She grumbles, giving Baku a scolding look.

I catch Ryu smirking in slight amusement behind Tama's back, but he looks uninclined to defend himself in this conversation.

"What makes you the sudden bastien of reason that you think you can question my judgment, Baku?" I speak up, irritation curling in my belly and making my voice come out cutting and icy.

Baku blinks at me, unaccustomed, I guess, to being on the receiving end of my displeasure.

"Did you really mark him? You completed the bond?" He wants to know.

I stare back at him defiantly and unashamed, "Yes, I did."

Baku swears and runs a hand through his hair, "You know what that means don't you? It's permanent, Rin. You'll never be able to be free of him even when he's in the pen."

"He's not going in the pen," I state firmly. Everyone in the room goes quiet.

I lick my lips nervously cause now all three of them are staring at me.

"What do you mean by that?" Baku demands.

I don't back down, and there's no taking it back now so I puff out my chest and tell them all what I've spent the last few hours deciding.

"Ryu won't be going in the pen. He's not going to be leaving my side at all. He's staying with me, here, unchained. I'm keeping him."

I didn't plan on announcing it this way, I didn't even really think the decision through much. It just came naturally, and now that I've voiced it and I'm more sure of it than I've ever been about anything before. Ryu's place is with me. He's not a threat to anyone, and even though I'm sure I'll get some push back for my decision and there will be risks, I'll figure it out. No one's going to be able to take him from me, and they can't force me to put him in a cage.

Both Baku and Tama look dumbfounded by this proclamation, but it's not their gazes I seek out. I've never spoken with Ryu about what happens after our confinement period ends, so there is genuine shock on his face as well.

"You can't be serious!" Baku whines, drawing my attention back to him.

"Baku," Tama warns, breaking out of her stunned trance.

"She can't do this," Baku continues, "It's unthinkable. A vanai walking around free, in a city full of humans? It's a disaster waiting to happen."

"He's not a danger to humans," I snap, starting to growl, "And he's been walking among them all day and not a single one of them noticed until you decided to start a fight."

Baku looks furious, "This can't happen. I'll go to the council, the others won't agree to this."

I curl my lips back and snarl, get ready to go for him again, "Then you'll deal with me. You won't get near him again without having to go through me."

Baku looks at me as though he's gazing at a stranger, "You'd turn your back on us? Over a monster?"

I'm milliseconds from going for his throat again, "He's not a monster. He's mine."

"Baku," Tama intercepts, her voice commanding our attention. Her eyes are hard on her brother and she speaks with more authority than I've ever heard from her before, "Drop it. Respect Rin's choices, what's done is done."

Baku gapes at her, "You can't expect me to be okay with this, surely?"

Tama's steely expression is impenetrable, "There is no threat here, stop insulting Rin's mate."

"He cannot be her true mate. He's vanai," Baku refutes.

"And so am I," I say, spine straightening with pride.

"You're going against your own kind!" Baku spits.

"Baku!" Tama shouts, louder, she's glowering now, eyes almost glowing with anger, "Enough. Leave."

Baku stares at her, I'm amazed by the exchange. I've seen Baku bicker with Tama plenty of times, but I've never seen him defy her, I've also never heard her give him an order with so much authority before. I think for a minute they might fight, but something maybe more ironically vanai wins out in Baku, and I can see him submitting. He doesn't look happy about it, but he blows out an angry breath, shoots me a look of betrayal, and stomps out, slamming the door shut behind him.

Tama sighs, shaking her head, then she nods at me and even Ryu, who's been silent and oddly blank ever since my impromptu announcement.

"I'm sorry for him. He will not cause trouble, I'll make sure of it," She swears, I relax a bit when she reaches out and puts a hand on my shoulder.

She says in a quieter voice so that only I can hear, though I suspect Ryu hears it anyway, "You look alive now, and happy. I'd didn't believe you before, but now I see you two together and the way he looks at you," She darts a quick glance at Ryu, "And I think there's no way that can be faked. I'm happy for you, and I'll do whatever I can to help you protect that happiness."

I smile at her, deeply grateful, "Thank you. I hope you find it too."

She smirks at that, like she doubts it, but she says nothing. She gives Ryu another acknowledging dip of her head as she turns toward the door, a purposefully respectful gesture that surprises me. I stare at the door as she closes it behind her. It takes several seconds for me to gather my thoughts and enough nerve to look at Ryu.

His blank expression is gone by the time I turn to him, he's replaced it with a small smile and a glitter in his eye that has my stomach fluttering wildly with butterflies.

"Decided to keep me, have you?" He asks, fangs flashing.

I return the smile with one of my own. He crosses the room and holds my face in his hands as he dips down and places his mouth over mine. The butterflies are in full flight when he lets go to press his brow to mine.

"I would've stepped in," he says, "But I have to admit, it was extremely attractive to watch you defend me. My fierce little mate."

I scoff and nip at his lips, "I just didn't want Baku leaving scratches on you with his *baby fangs*."

Ryu bubbles with laughter, but he also stares down into my eyes with an intensity that leaves me breathless.

"Did you mean what you said to him?" Ryu asks.

I don't need him to clarify which part, I just nod, "You're mine," I confirm, feeling the rightness of the statement in every bone of my body.

Ryu scoops me up, he must've scoped out where my bed was located sometime during the exchange, because he doesn't need my direction to find it. Even though I'm the one who staked the claim on him, as Ryu lays me down and works his way down my body, it feels very much like I'm as much his as he is mine.

Epilogue

"Is this okay?" Ryu asks, leaning to one side to give me access as I slip my finger beneath the metal collar around his neck to hold it in place.

It's been two weeks since our confinement officially ended, and though there has been some uproar over my decision to keep Ryu out of the pen, in the end, the council was unwilling to press the issue. A lot of the other halflings were upset by it, but the girls from Uthon came around rather quickly. Like me, they haven't spent their whole lives exposed to vanai and the matings, so they are not as prejudiced against the vanai as the halflings born in Songak. They want to know all about Ryu, and listened with fascination when I told them the truth about the bond.

I'm not sure they all believe me yet, but they have been welcoming toward Ryu, once they saw that he was not aggressive or threatening like they thought he would be. Baku has remained repulsed by the whole thing, but Aksha is slowly starting to accept Ryu's frequent presence.

We're being left alone, but the peace is tentative, and I know it's not permanent. There will be problems, if not with us then with the other Uthon halflings when it comes time for them to figure out where they stand on the treatment of the vanai. The halflings in the city recognize Ryu when we're out and regard him with disdain, though they keep their distance. The humans for the most part don't notice the difference, but the presence of his collar always makes me nervous lest someone notices.

I suggested to Ryu that we could relocate to Uthon after the confinement, where there is more space and more places for us to have privacy and be away from humans. I'm even a little curious if we could go to the vanai city so I can see it for myself. Ryu refused, he thinks I have a purpose here and that the citizens of Songak need more halflings to protect them, including any children we might have. So I need to make our lives here safer.

This is my solution, and Ryu still looked skeptical when I returned this afternoon with the key to his collar. He's been getting better about being comfortable with me leaving to run errands alone for short periods. I can see he doesn't buy my explanation that I was able to talk someone into letting me remove his collar.

I, however, have stopped believing I need the council's permission to do anything. And they made finding the key way too easy, it's almost like they wanted me to take it.

"It will make me feel better," I say, "Without this, the humans won't be able to tell you apart from the halfbloods."

HALFBLOOD

I fit the key into the lock and turn. The collar comes apart with a click and I take it and toss it into a corner of the room, never to be thought about again. Ryu is free, and I watch him rise to his full height with pride. The neck of his robes finally looks right without the ugly metal collar. I relish his beaming smile as he looks at himself in the mirror as well. He is the most beautiful creature I've ever seen, and he might've just changed the future for more of his kind unintentionally. Whatever else he may be, he's mine first, and as he takes my hand and we head out for our afternoon walk, I feel safe, and I know we'll figure it all out.

The End

About the Author

AN Kim is a loving dog owner, okay wife, averagely decent mother, and sometimes chooses to identify as an Asian-American author. After traveling between her hometown in Illinois to Thailand all of her youth, she now resides nowhere near either in Northern Washington state. When not balancing the intricate details of running a multi-cultural and multi-lingual household; you can often find her in her backyard, talking to her chickens. She also sometimes enjoys writing scandalously filthy smut featuring diverse characters that may involve multiple threesomes.